P9-DBK-940

DIVINE AND HUMAN

AND OTHER STORIES BY
LEO TOLSTOY

DIVINE AND HUMAN

AND OTHER STORIES BY
LEO TOLSTOY

ZondervanPublishingHouse
Grand Rapids, Michigan

A Division of HarperCollinsPublishers

NEW TRANSLATIONS BY PETER SEKIRIN

Divine and Human
Copyright © 2000 by Peter Sekirin

Requests for information should be addressed to:

ZondervanPublishingHouse
Grand Rapids, Michigan 49530

Library of Congress Cataloging-in-Publication Data

Tolstoy, Leo, graf, 1828–1910.
    [Short stories. English. Selections]
    Divine and human and other stories / by Leo Tolstoy; new translations by
Peter Sekirin.
       p. cm.
    ISBN: 0-310-22367-9
      1. Tolstoy, Leo, graf, 1828–1910—Translations into English. 2. Christian
fiction, Russian—Translations into English. I. Title: Divine and human. II.
Sekirin, Peter. III. Title.
PG3366.A13 S45 2000
891.73'3-dc21   00-020791
                                                              CIP

This edition is printed on acid-free paper.

All rights reserved. No part of this publication may be reproduced, stored in a
retrieval system, or transmitted in any form or by any means—electronic,
mechanical, photocopy, recording, or any other—except for brief quotations in
printed reviews, without the prior permission of the publisher.

Printed in the United States of America

00 01 02 03 04 05 06 /❖ DC/ 10 9 8 7 6 5 4 3 2 1

Contents

ACKNOWLEDGMENTS

I would like to express my deepest and most sincere gratitude to the following people:

My editors at Zondervan, Dave Lambert and Lori Vanden Bosch, as well as Janet Wehrle, who reviewed the translation;

My agent, Ivy Stone, at Fifi Oscard Agency;

My friends and colleagues who read the manuscript: Kim Yates, Chet Scoville, Colman Hogan, Melissa Temerty, and Mark Crimmins;

My parents, Vera and Vsevolod Sekirin.

This book became a reality due to their tireless assistance, support, and encouragement.

TRANSLATOR'S PREFACE

The stories in this book were originally published at the very beginning of the twentieth century as part of a larger work, *The Circle of Reading (Krug Chteniia)*, which consisted of two volumes. The first of those was *The Thoughts of Wise People;* my English translation of that volume, *The Calendar of Wisdom*, was published by Scribner in 1997. It is the second volume, *The Sunday Reading Stories*, from which these stories were selected. That book consists of fifty-two weekly readings, including more than thirty stories and essays by Tolstoy himself, which are mostly unknown to the English-speaking reader ("Kornei Vasiliev," "Why Did It Happen?", "The Prayer," and others), as well as Tolstoy's adaptations of stories and essays by Victor Hugo, Kant, Pascal, Chekhov, and other writers. For *Divine and Human*, we have selected predominantly works of fiction by Tolstoy, most of them appearing here in English translation for the first time, as well as a small number of retellings by Tolstoy of the works of others, such as "The Poor People" (from Hugo) and "Sisters" (from Maupassant).

Tolstoy considered *The Circle of Reading* to be the major work of his life. Considering its difficult history, it is not surprising that only recently has it been rediscovered and that only now is it being published in English for the first time.

Tolstoy created the work in 1901–03, after many years of meditation about the meaning of life, as a collection of "the best examples of Christian literature." The book enjoyed huge popularity, with three revised editions from 1903–12. In spite of this success, it was heavily censored and suppressed by the Tsarist government because of its strong pacifism and criticism of the monarchy; a few years later, it was similarly suppressed by Soviet authorities, this time because of its many religious quotes and references.

Leo Tolstoy considered this book as "the most important" of all his works. He constantly kept it on his writing desk during the last five years of his life, highly recommended it to his friends, and repeatedly read it to his family.

Several hours before his death, Tolstoy asked his assistant to bring him a Bible, *The Works of Shakespeare*, and the last edition of this book. It is highly significant and symbolic that Leo Tolstoy used this book as the final guide in his own search for truth, the meaning of life, and spiritual revival.

FOREWORD

Leo Tolstoy completed his last major work just before his escape from Yasnaya Polyana and his death in the small railway station of Astapovo, deep in the heart of Russia. This work began with Tolstoy's compilation *The Thoughts of Wise People*, and continued with *The Circle of Reading, Thoughts for Every Day*, and finally, *The Way of Life*, which was published in 1910.

The Circle of Reading consists of two closely interconnected volumes. The first volume, *The Thoughts of Wise People*, was published recently in English under the title *A Calendar of Wisdom* (Scribner, 1997). It is a collection of the thoughts of the greatest philosophers and writers throughout history, thematically arranged as a series of daily readings.

The second volume was *The Sunday Reading Stories*, a collection of short stories and essays linked with the readings in *The Calendar of Wisdom* for each week of the year. Some of the stories were written by Tolstoy himself, and some were translated or simply borrowed by Tolstoy from his favorite authors: Socrates, Pascal, Dostoyevsky, and Victor Hugo, among others.

The stories in the collection you hold in your hand were selected from *The Sunday Reading Stories*. Because this last great volume of Tolstoy's work has been neglected for so long, most of the stories in *Divine and Human* are appearing in English for the first time.

This major work, which occupied the last ten years of Tolstoy's life, documents the development of his thought during this period. He began by collecting "wise thoughts" and stories representing "the best achievements of Christian literature" by other authors, and gradually moved toward the creation of his own thoughts and literary pieces.

The collection *The Thoughts of Wise People* thus became the starting point and foundation for his own views on philosophy, ethics, and aesthetics. In this wide-ranging collection of the works and thoughts of numerous philosophers, writers, and historical and religious figures, the reader can see in Tolstoy's interpretations the maturation of his own thoughts. *The Circle of Reading* is therefore unique in that it can be read in both artistic and philosophical terms as an original work by Leo Tolstoy.

During the Soviet period, *The Circle of Reading* was not included in official editions of Tolstoy's works. It stands, along with the brilliant pamphlet "I Cannot Remain Silent," which was also omitted by Soviet censors from the most recent twenty-two-volume edition of Tolstoy's works, as one of the great artistic and philosophical triumphs of the twentieth century. It is one of Tolstoy's major works—a work that has until now not been well understood or appreciated.

The long critical neglect of *The Circle of Reading* can also be understood as a result of textual scholarship that ignored the larger context of Tolstoy's literary heritage of world philosophy and non-Russian literature, a vitally important factor in his creative and philosophical outlook. Tolstoy worked consciously within the context of world literature, and it is necessary to understand that this literary heritage contributed generously to his creative process.

A few Tolstoy scholars have treated *The Circle of Reading* secondarily, as merely "an encyclopedia of Tolstoyism." This approach is unfair, both to Tolstoy and his work. *The Circle of Reading* is much wider and more humane than this so-called "tolstovsto." We find in it a genre of philosophical prose that did not exist in Russian literature before Tolstoy. One cannot justly state that *Evgeny Onegin* is "an encyclopedia of Pushkinism," because it is more accurately a survey of the totality of Russian life and the Russian outlook of its time. *The Circle of Reading* stands likewise as an encyclopedia of human civilization, of all-embracing thoughts on mankind, life and death, God, religion, art, and literature.

Tolstoy considered art to be a means of unification for all peoples and nations, and that belief resulted in his drive to collect the works and thoughts of so many authors. World literature, for Tolstoy, became an avenue for the unification of all humanity.

On March 6, 1884, Tolstoy wrote to Nikolai Gusev, his assistant, that he was busy collecting and translating wise thoughts and works by philosophers and writers from all times and peoples. This is the first time Tolstoy recorded a reference to the concept of *The Circle of Reading*. On March 15 in the same year, he wrote in his diary:

> I have to make a circle of reading for myself: Epictetus, Marcus Aurelius, Lao-Tse, Buddha, Pascal, the New Testament. This is necessary for all. (*Complete Works in Ninety Volumes*, vol. 49, p. 68)

Although the plan for this work first appeared in the mid 1880s, evidence of Tolstoy's search for moral truth and the meaning of life appears first in his early daybooks, and is evident in his writing throughout life. During every period of his life, Tolstoy tried to understand and to define the notion of God. In the summer of 1906, he wrote in his notebook:

> Does God exist? I don't know. I know that there is a law for my spiritual being, and I call the source and cause of this law, God. (vol. 55, p. 380)

On October 16 of that year, he formulated the thought more clearly:

> I understand by "God" that being, a part of which I understand, in my limited state, as God. (vol. 56, p. 383)

The comprehension of the divine forms only one side of Tolstoy's search for truth—faith (not only religious faith) is the major principle of Tolstoy's general outlook. Faith is also the passionate assurance of the ideals of goodness and justice which form the basis of all of Tolstoy's thought. He expressed this very clearly in *The Circle of Reading:*

> This is one of the prejudices ... that a person can live without faith. At all times, people tried to have ... one common purpose. (Jan. 2)

Christianity has, throughout most of its history, been the basis of the development of the Russian culture, and this idea permeates *The Circle of Reading.*

❧

Tolstoy considered *The Circle of Reading* to be the most important book of his whole life. "One can live without many books, including the other works of Tolstoy," he said, "but one cannot live without *The Circle of Reading.*" His assistant, N. Gusev, wrote in his daybook on May 16, 1908:

> Yesterday Lev Nikolaevich told me, "I cannot understand why people do not widely use *The Circle of Reading* in their lives. What could be more precious than to communicate with the wisest people of the whole world?" Tolstoy added, "What a good book! When I put it together, and every time I read it, I reach new spiritual heights."

When Tolstoy embarked upon his last journey, from Shamardino to the railway station at Astapovo, he took a copy of *The Circle of Reading* from his sister, a nun at the Shamardino monastery. It was the last book he read.

❧

Tolstoy's interest in collections of wisdom literature was sparked in 1886, when he compiled *A Calendar of Proverbs for 1887* for the Posrednik Publishers. This interest shaped the genre of *The Circle of Reading,* a work that was philosophical and at the same time deeply artistic in nature, clearly connected with Tolstoy's earlier works. A connective link between philosophy and fiction was forged in *The Weekly Readings* (a different title for *The Sunday Reading Stories*) as well as in *The Monthly Readings,* which existed only in draft version.

During Tolstoy's serious illness in December 1902, he began to plan his future work, and in January 1903, he started to collect the materials for this book. The result was *The Thoughts of Wise People,* which was published in August 1903 by Posrednik Publishers. A copy was presented to Tolstoy for his 75th birthday on August 28, 1903. Ivan Bunin wrote in *The Liberation of Tolstoy:*

> He included in this book pieces and wise thoughts by different writers from many countries, people and times, as well as those written by himself.

In the following years, the book went through several revised editions. Tolstoy was unsatisfied with the first edition, and in January 1906 he began a new edition of *The Thoughts of Wise People,* but it was left unfinished because he became involved with a new project, *The Circle of Reading.* A comparison of *The Thoughts of Wise People* and *The Circle of Reading* with the two books that followed, *For Each Day* and *The Way of Life,* demonstrates that Tolstoy included more and more of his own writings in each successive publication. *The Thoughts of Wise People* contains only a few of Tolstoy's own pieces, but the last book in the series, *The Way of Life,* is entirely reorganized: it contains only a few pieces by other authors, and the bulk of the writing is Tolstoy's.

Nevertheless, in his introductions to several of the editions of *The Way of Life,* Tolstoy felt obliged to write:

> Most of these thoughts, during both the translation and editing, have undergone so many changes that I consider it neither necessary nor suitable to place the names of their original authors under them. The best of these

unfinished thoughts do not belong to me, but to the greatest thinkers of the world. (vol. 45, p. 17)

Tolstoy began working on *The Circle of Reading* in January 1904, when he decided to revise *The Thoughts of Wise People*. He worked at this book with great passion, as expressed in his 1906 diary entry: "It is a joyful book." N. Gusev recalled that, during his work on *The Circle of Reading*, Tolstoy came to the breakfast table one morning and said, "I had a wonderful time and enjoyed a great company: Socrates, Rousseau, Kant, and Amiel." He then added that he was greatly surprised at how people could ignore these great thinkers in favor of the tasteless and thoughtless books of his popular contemporaries, saying, "It is just the same as a man who, on being offered a healthy and nutritious meal, prefers to root in the garbage for dirty trash, potato peels, and rotted waste, and tries to eat this instead."

Tolstoy was greatly surprised by the "lack of culture which embraces society," and he repeatedly stressed that "real education should use and assimilate the spiritual heritage left by previous generations."

The first edition of *The Circle of Reading* was published in three volumes, which appeared in February, July, and October of 1905. In August 1907, Tolstoy prepared a new and revised edition of the book for publication, which he submitted to his publisher, I. Sytin, in January 1908. Later that year Tolstoy read the galleys of the new edition, but the book was not published. N. Gusev explained the unwillingness of the editors to publish this book: "Sytin delayed the publication because he was afraid of a court case."

After a court decision, twelve sections were deleted from the book: thoughts on private property by Henry George; on the state by Tolstoy; on the ownership of land by Tolstoy and Black Hawk; on the liberation of people by Mazzini; on war (two sections) by Tolstoy; two readings by Peter Khelchitsky, an early Czech religious thinker who wrote *The Network of Faith*; and one of Tolstoy's weekly stories, "Harrison and His Proclamation." *The Circle of Reading* was eventually published in abbreviated form in 1911 by V. Sablin, and appears in this form in the *Works of Leo Tolstoy*, volumes 11–17. The publisher Sytin finally issued a second edition of *The Circle of Reading* in 1911–12, in which the cuts made by the censors were even deeper and more numerous than those in the first edition.

In September 1907, Tolstoy had begun work on a new anthology, *For Each Day*, which was essentially a new version of *The Circle of Reading*. In 1910, before he completed this book, he began work on another new project, *The Way of Life*, which was completed a month before his death and published by the Posrednik Publishers in 1911 in eleven small volumes. J. Gorbunov-Posadov, the publisher of this edition, recollected that Tolstoy was planning to continue his work on *The Way of Life* in order "to make them even more simple and accessible for each and every person." Only death prevented Tolstoy from completing this "joyful work."

Tolstoy commented on the progress of his work at the time in his introduction to *The Circle of Reading*, stating that his translations were often not directly from the language of the original, and that as a result, his translations "were not necessarily close to the originals." Tolstoy often edited texts heavily during his work—shortening, deleting words and sometimes whole sentences that he thought made a weak impression, and sometimes even adding phrases of his own when he thought that these changes would make the message more powerful or easier to comprehend.

This approach reflected Tolstoy's theoretical views on the issue of translation: he translated what he understood to be the superior truth, rather than a word-for-word rendering of a piece. He wrote to V. Chertkov on February 22, 1886:

> We should interpret the original as freely as possible, placing God's truth ahead of the name of any particular author.

Tolstoy's introduction concluded with the following thought: "If someone will translate this book into other languages, do this not from the languages of the originals, but from my text" (vol. 42,

p. 473). In order to better understand the major message of the book—"it can, and must be continuous joy"—we may quote Tolstoy's diary of October 1, 1892:

> It is a strange thing to think and to say, that the purpose of our lives is either to reproduce the species, or to continue the family, or to serve mankind, or to serve God. This is all wrong. To what purpose do we reproduce our species? To what end might we serve mankind? And what should those people whom we serve do? To serve God? He can do all He needs to do without our help. And He does not need anything. Even if He orders us to serve Him, it is only for our own sake, for our own good. Life cannot have any purpose other than joy and goodness. Only this purpose—joy—is ultimately worthy of life. (vol. 52, p. 73)

After the completion of his work on *The Circle of Reading*, Tolstoy wrote in his diary on January 21, 1905:

> I have just noticed how I have descended from that spiritual, moral height which I achieved by communicating with the best and wisest people, whom I read and whose thoughts I meditated upon while working at my *Circle of Reading*. (vol. 55, p. 120)

Once, the Tolstoy Museum in Moscow had an old visitor, a man who had spent much of his life in Stalin's prison camps during the decades of purges, terror, and repression. He said that he had survived only because he had read and remembered *The Circle of Reading*. There are only a few books in the world that have so much life-giving power. In the midst of a sea of evil and cruelty, Tolstoy's last book appealed to kindness, humanity, and God.

ALEXANDER NIKOLIUKIN
Moscow

About the Stories

The Son of a Thief. Tolstoy's free interpretation of a story by Nikolai Leskov, "Abused Before Christmas," published in the *St. Petersburg Gazette* on December 25, 1890, and sent immediately after by the author to Tolstoy. The story was not included in Leskov's *Works* or anthologized in book form.

The Repentant Sinner. A tale written by Tolstoy in 1886 and included in *The Circle of Reading* exactly as he had originally written it.

The Archangel Gabriel. Originally written by the Persian poet F. Attar, translated and reinterpreted by Tolstoy.

The Prayer. The plot of this story was borrowed by Tolstoy from the peasant storyteller V. Shchlegolenok, who visited Yasnaya Polyana, Tolstoy's estate, in 1879. First published in *The Circle of Reading*. This was Tolstoy's response to a shipwreck in the United States that caused the death of many children.

The Poor People. Tolstoy's prosaic retelling of a poem by Victor Hugo, from the book *Legends of the Centuries*. Hugo's poem was originally translated into Russian by L. Veselitskaya (pen name: V. Mikulich) and later retold and edited by Tolstoy. In his famous essay "What Is Art?" Tolstoy said, "This story by Hugo is an example of the highest religious art based on love to God and your neighbor."

A Coffeehouse in the City of Surat. Written by Tolstoy in 1887. This story is one of the few in the book that has appeared previously in English. It was first published in English in 1901.

Kornei Vasiliev. Written by Tolstoy in February of 1905.

A Grain of Rye the Size of a Chicken Egg. Written by Tolstoy in 1886.

The Berries. Written by Tolstoy on June 10–11, 1905.

Stones. A fable adapted by Tolstoy from the collection *Antony Alexeevich, A Hermit from Don*, by E. Poselianin.

The Big Dipper. Tolstoy's free translation of a tale published in *The Herald of Peace*, a British journal.

The Power of Childhood. Tolstoy's free adaptation of the story "The Civil War" by Victor Hugo. Tolstoy dictated this version into a dictating phonograph after having read Hugo's story the day before.

Why Did It Happen? This story by Tolstoy is based on a case documented in the book *Siberia and Its Prisons* by S. Maximov.

Divine and Human. A novella by Tolstoy suggested by the book *The Underground Russia* by S. Stepniak-Kravchinsky. It was originally written as a chapter in *Resurrection* (but removed by Tolstoy from that manuscript before *Resurrection* was published), then rewritten and expanded to stand alone.

The Requirements of Love. An excerpt from Tolstoy's diary, dated June 25, 1893.

Sisters. A story by Tolstoy based on the story "In the Port" by Maupassant.

THE SON
OF A
THIEF

The Son of a Thief

One day the city court convened for a jury trial. Among the members of the jury were peasants, noblemen, and salesmen. The foreman of the jury was a merchant, Ivan Akimovich Belov, respected and loved by everyone for his good life: he led his business honestly, never cheated anyone, and helped others. He was an old man, in his late sixties. The members of the jury came into the courtroom, took the oath, and took their places. The defendant was brought in, a horse-thief who had stolen a horse from a peasant. But as they started the court proceedings, Ivan Akimovich stood and said, "Excuse me, your honor, but I cannot be a member of the jury."

The judge was surprised. "Why is this?"

"I simply can't. Please let me go."

And suddenly Ivan Akimovich's voice trembled, and he began to cry. He cried and cried, so hard that he couldn't even speak. When he regained control of himself, he said to the judge, "I can't be on this jury, your honor, because my father and I were perhaps worse than this thief. How could I judge someone guilty of the same kind of evil as I am? I can't do this. I ask you, please—let me go."

The judge let Ivan Akimovich go. That night, the judge invited Ivan Akimovich to his house and asked him a question: "Why did you refuse to be a juror?"

"Here's why," said Ivan Akimovich, and told the following story:

You think that I am a merchant's son and that I was born in your city. That's not true. I am a peasant's son. My father was a peasant, but he was also a thief, the best thief in the neighborhood, and he died in prison. He was a kind man, but he drank, and when he was drunk, he beat my mother, became violent, and was capable of all kinds of evil deeds, and then he would repent.

One day he enticed me to steal, and on that day my happiness came to an end. My father was with other thieves in a pub, and they started to talk about where they could steal something. My father said, "Listen, fellows. You know the merchant Belov's storehouse that faces the street. There are lots of expensive goods in this storehouse. It is hard to get inside, but I have a plan. And here's my plan: There is a small window in the storehouse, high above the ground and too narrow for an adult to get inside. But here's what I think. I have a boy, and he is a very smart boy indeed," he said, about me. "We'll tie a rope around him and hoist him up to the window. Once he is inside, we'll lower him down to the storehouse floor. Then we'll give him another rope, and he'll tie the expensive goods from the storehouse onto it, and we will pull it down. And when we've taken as much as we can carry, then we'll pull him out, too."

The thieves liked this idea and they said, "Well then, bring your son here."

So my father came home and asked for me. My mother said, "What do you want him for?"

"What difference does it make? I need him."

My mother said, "He's outside."

"Call him inside."

My mother knew that when he was drunk she couldn't argue with him or he would beat her. She ran outside and called me into the house. My father asked me, "Vanka, are you good at climbing fences?"

"Oh, yes, I can climb anywhere."

"Then come with me."

My mother tried to talk him out of it, but he threatened to hit her and she became quiet. My father put on my coat and off we went to the pub; they gave me tea with sugar and some snacks, and we sat until night came. When it was dark, all of us—there were three men—went out.

We came to the merchant Belov's storehouse. Right away they tied a rope around me, gave me the other rope, and hoisted me up. "Aren't you afraid?" they asked me.

"Why should I be afraid? I'm not afraid of anything."

"Then get inside and get hold of the best thing you can find there. Find some furs, and tie them up with the rope you're holding. Make sure you tie the things to the middle of the rope, and not to the end, so that when we pull it out, your end of the rope will stay inside with you. Do you understand?" they asked.

Of course I understood. How could I not understand such simple things?

So they helped me up to the window, I climbed in, and they lowered me to the floor with the rope. As soon as I felt something solid under my feet, I began to feel around with my hands. It was so dark I couldn't see a thing. When I felt something furry, I fixed it to the rope—not to the end but to the middle—and they pulled it out. Then I pulled the rope back to me and tied more goods to it.

When we had done this about three times, they pulled all the rope to themselves. This meant enough. Then they started to pull me back out the window, while I held the rope with my small hands. They had pulled me only about halfway when—boom!—the rope went slack, and I fell. It was good that I fell on cushions, and was not hurt.

Afterwards, I found out what had happened: a guard saw my father and the other thieves, gave an alarm, and they let go of the rope and ran away with the stolen things, leaving me by myself.

Lying alone in the darkness, I became terrified. "Mommy!" I cried. "Mommy, Mommy, Mommy!" I was so tired from crying, fear, and lack of sleep that I don't remember how I finally drifted off to sleep on the cushions.

I awoke suddenly and saw in front of me the man who owned the storehouse, the merchant Belov, with a lantern and a police officer. The policeman asked me who had brought me there. I said, "My father."

"And who is your father?"

At that, I started to cry all over again.

Belov was an old man, and he said to the policeman, "God be with him. A child is the soul of God. It is not good to witness against your own father. What's been stolen is stolen."

Belov was a good man, God rest his soul. And his wife was even kinder than he. She took me to her room and gave me some gifts, and I stopped crying. As you know, a child can be made happy with small things. In the morning, she asked me, "Do you want to go home?"

Not knowing what to say, I said, "Yes, I do."

"And would you like to stay with me here?" she asked.

"Yes," I said, "I would."

"Then stay with me."

And so I stayed, living at their home with them. They did the necessary paperwork to make me their foster child. First I worked at the shop as a delivery boy. When I grew up, they made me a shop assistant, and later, a shop manager. I worked hard. They were very kind people, and they loved me and allowed me to marry their daughter. They treated me as if I were their son. When the old man died, all his estate went to me.

"And that is who I am," concluded Ivan Akimovich. "I am a thief and the son of a thief, and I cannot judge others. To do so is not a Christian thing, your honor. We should forgive other people and love them. If a person has made a mistake, you should not punish him but rather take pity, remembering what Christ told us."

That was the story of Ivan Akimovich.

And the judge stopped asking questions and considered whether, according to the laws of Christ, it was possible to judge others.

THE
REPENTANT
SINNER

The Repentant Sinner

And he said unto Jesus, Lord, remember me when thou comest into thy kingdom. And Jesus said unto him, Verily I say unto thee, Today shalt thou be with me in paradise.

LUKE 32:42–43

Once there was a man who had lived in sin for all of his seventy years. One day he fell ill, but even then he did not confess his sins. When death came, he cried out in the last hour of his life, saying, "Oh my God, forgive me, as you forgave the robber on the cross!" As soon as he had said this, his soul departed. His soul dwelt in the love and mercy of the Lord, and soon came to the doors of paradise.

And the sinner knocked at the door and asked to be granted entrance into the kingdom of heaven.

And he heard a voice from behind the door say, "Who is knocking at the door of paradise, and what deeds has this man committed during his life?"

And another voice, the voice of the accuser, listed all the man's sins, and mentioned not a single good deed.

And the first voice behind the door answered, "Sinners cannot enter the kingdom of God. Depart from here."

And the man said, "Oh Lord, I hear your voice, but I cannot see your face, and I do not know your name."

And the voice answered, "I am the apostle Peter."

And the sinner said, "Please forgive me, Peter the apostle, and remember human weakness and the mercy of God. Weren't you a disciple of Christ? Weren't you the same man who heard the teachings of Christ from his own lips and observed the example of his life? And don't you remember, when he missed you and grieved for you with all his soul, how he asked you three times to pray and not fall asleep, but you slept because your eyes were heavy, and three times he found you sleeping? So it is with me.

"And do you remember how you promised to be with him until the end, but then you rejected him three times when they brought him to Caiaphas? So it is with me.

"And do you remember how, when the rooster crowed in the morning, you went out and wept bitterly? So it is with me. Therefore, you cannot refuse me entrance."

And the voice behind the door disappeared.

And the man waited a little while, and again knocked at the door and asked to be granted entrance to the kingdom of heaven.

And he heard another voice from behind the door, and it said, "Who is this man, and how has he lived his life on earth?"

And again the accuser named each of the sins of the sinner, without mentioning a single good deed.

And the voice from behind the door answered, "Depart from here! Such sinners cannot live with us in paradise."

And the sinner said, "Lord, I hear your voice, but I cannot see your face, and I do not know your name."

And the voice replied, "I am David, the king and prophet."

And the sinner did not despair; he remained before the doors of paradise, and said, "Take pity on me, King David, and remember the weakness of humanity and the mercy of God. God loved you and exalted you before men. You had everything: a kingdom, and glory, and wealth, and wives, and children; but from your roof you saw the wife of a poor man and became filled with sin. You took Uriah's wife, and you had him killed by the swords of the Ammonites. You were a wealthy man, yet you took the last sheep of a poor man, and murdered him. So did I. And yet after this you repented of your sin and said, 'I confess my guilt and am grieved over my sin.' So it is with me. You cannot refuse me entrance."

And the voice behind the door disappeared.

And again the man waited for a little while, and again he knocked at the door and asked to enter the kingdom of heaven. And a third voice was heard from behind the door which said, "Who is this man, and how did he live his life on earth?"

And for the third time, the accuser named all the misdeeds of the sinner, without mentioning a single good thing.

And this third voice from behind the door answered, "Depart from here! Sinners can never enter the kingdom of God."

The sinner said, "I hear your voice, but I cannot see your face, and I do not know your name."

The voice replied, "I am John, Christ's beloved disciple."

And the sinner rejoiced and said, "Now you *cannot* refuse me entrance. Peter and David will let me in because they understand human weakness and the mercy of God. And you must allow me to enter because you are filled with love. Wasn't it you, John, who wrote in your book that God is love and that those who have not love do not know God? When you grew old, wasn't it you who said to people only the phrase, 'Brothers, love one another!' How can you, after all of that, hate me and leave me outside? You must either denounce everything you taught or love me and grant me entrance into the kingdom of God."

And the gates of paradise opened, and John embraced the repentant sinner, and welcomed him into the kingdom of heaven.

THE
ARCHANGEL
GABRIEL

THE ARCHANGEL GABRIEL

Once upon a time, the archangel Gabriel heard the voice of God speaking from paradise, blessing someone. Gabriel said, "Surely this is some important servant of my Lord, God the Father. He must be a great saint, or hermit, or wise man."

The archangel went down to earth looking for the man, but he could not find him, neither on earth nor in heaven. Then he addressed God and said, "Oh Lord, my God, please show me how to find the object of your love."

God answered him, "Go to this village. And there, in a little temple, you will see a fire."

The angel went down to the temple, and he found a man praying before an idol. Then he went back to God and said, "Lord, how can you look with love upon this idol worshiper?"

God said, "It is true that he does not understand me properly. Not one man living is capable of understanding me as I am. The wisest of the whole human race are just as far from really understanding me as this man is. I look not at his mind, but at his heart. The heart of this man searches for me, and therefore he is close to me."

THE
PRAYER

The Prayer

"No, no, no, this can't be! Doctor, is it true that we can do nothing? Why are you silent?"

So said the young mother, walking with long, resolute steps from the nursery where a three-year-old boy, her first and only son, was dying of dropsy.

Her husband and the doctor, who had been conversing in low voices, grew silent. Her husband approached timidly; tenderly, he brushed his hand over her disheveled hair and sighed deeply. The doctor stood with his head bowed, his silence an expression of the hopelessness of the situation.

"What can we do?" said the husband. "What can we do, my dear?"

"Oh, don't say it, don't say it!" she cried reproachfully. Turning her back to him, she walked quickly back toward the nursery.

Her husband wanted to stop her. "Katya, please don't go."

Without answering, she looked at him with big, tired eyes and returned to the nursery.

The boy lay in the arms of his nursemaid, with a white pillow under his head. His eyes were open but sightless. Foam bubbled between the pressed lips of his small mouth. The old servant watched with a very strict and solemn expression, as if she were looking somewhere beyond him. She made no movement when the mother entered. When the mother came closer and put her hand under the pillow to take the baby, the nursemaid said quietly, "He is leaving us," and tried to turn away from the mother.

But the mother didn't listen. With a familiar movement, she took the boy into her arms. His long, curly hair was tangled. She combed it with her fingers and looked into his face. "No, no, I can't," she whispered. Hurriedly, she gave the boy back to the nursemaid and left the room.

The boy had been ill for two weeks. During his sickness, his mother had vacillated between desperation and hope, sleeping barely an hour and a half each night. Several times a day, she went into her bedroom, knelt in front of the huge icon of the Savior with his golden robes, and prayed that God would save her boy. The dark-faced Savior held in his small, dark hand a golden book upon which was written in black letters, "Come to me all you who labor and are heavily burdened, and I will give you rest." Standing before this icon, she prayed, imbuing her prayer with all the power of her soul, although somewhere deep within her she feared that God would not move the mountain—that he would act not according to her desires, but according to his own will. Nevertheless, she continued to pray, reciting all the prayers she knew and composing her own, which she spoke aloud with special earnestness.

Now that she knew he was dead, she felt something happen in her head. It was as if something broke loose and started to spin, and when she returned to her bedroom, she looked at her things as if she didn't recognize the place. She then fell onto her bed and lost consciousness, with her head not on the pillow but on her husband's bathrobe.

In her sleep she can see her Kostya, happy, cheerful, healthy. He sits in a little armchair with his curly hair brushing his thin white neck and kicks his chubby feet in the air. Then he purses his lips and very carefully seats a small doll—a figure of a boy—on a toy horse that is missing a leg and has a hole in its back.

It is good that he is alive, she thinks. *And how cruel that he has died. Why, why would the God to whom I prayed so much allow him to die? Why? Did my boy bother anyone? Did he do anything bad to any-body? Doesn't God know that he was my whole life, that I can't live without him? And then to suddenly take and torture this helpless, inno-cent little creature and shatter my life and answer all my prayers with his lifeless eyes, with his cold, stiff body.*

And then she sees another scene. Now he walks, such a small boy, through tall, open doors, swinging his arms just as grown people do. She watches him, smiling.

My darling! And God wanted to torture him and kill him! Why pray to God if he can do such terrible things?

And then suddenly a young girl, Mary, the nurse's aide, is say-ing something strange. The mother knows that this is Mary—but she is at the same time both Mary and an angel. *If she is an angel, why doesn't she have wings on her back?* wonders the mother. Then she recalls that someone—she doesn't remember who, but it was someone she trusted—once told her that some angels don't have wings these days. And Mary the angel says, "You should not be angry with God. He cannot listen to everyone. Sometimes people hear only one side, and in order to do good for one, the other is abused. For example, right now, people all over Russia are praying to God. All kinds of people! Bishops and monks are praying in front of relics in cathedrals, and they pray for one thing—that God will grant Russia victory over the Japanese. But is this a good thing? You cannot pray for such things; God cannot grant the requests of everyone. The Japanese people also pray for victory, but, you see, there is only one Father of us all. What should he do? What should he do, my lady?" asks Mary.

"Yes, what you say is true," the mother replies. "It is nothing new. Even the French philosopher Voltaire talked about it. But still I ask: Why could God not fulfill my request, when I asked him not for something evil, but only not to kill my dear little boy? I cannot live without him!" The mother feels how he hugs her neck with his plump hands, and then she feels the warmth of his little body against her own. *It is good that this didn't happen,* she thinks.

"Yes, but this is not the same, my lady," Mary says in her incoherent manner. "This is not the same at all. Sometimes a person prays for something impossible, a request that cannot be fulfilled. And this we know for sure. It is because I know about this that I am telling you about it," Mary says, speaking in the same tone of voice she used yesterday when saying to the nursemaid, "I am sure that the master is home."

"How many times have I said that here is a good young man," continues Mary. "He prays for help to stay out of trouble, to avoid drunkenness and debauchery. He prays that these vices would be removed from him."

Mary speaks so beautifully, thinks the mistress.

"But it is quite impossible for him to have what he asks for, because everyone should make an effort in this life. Only when you make an effort is there goodness in this world.

"You yourself, my lady, gave me the book of fairy tales to read, the one about the black hen who gave a magic hemp seed to a boy for saving her life. As long as he kept it in the pocket of his trousers, he knew all his lessons without doing his homework. Because he had this seed, he completely stopped studying and forgot everything he knew. So God cannot remove evil from people. And you should not ask God for this, because you need to pull the evil out of yourself."

How does she know all this? wonders the mistress, and says, "All the same, Mary, you have not answered my question."

"Allow me enough time and I will tell you everything," replies Mary. "Sometimes it happens like this: Without being guilty of anything, a family can become bankrupt, lose their business, and, instead of a good apartment, live in some dirty room. They don't even have money to buy tea! They all weep, praying for some kind of help. God could satisfy all of their prayers, but he knows that it wouldn't be good for them. They don't see it, but the Father knows that if they lived in luxury with lots of money, they would become completely spoiled."

This is true, thinks the mistress. *But why does she speak about God in such a vulgar way? It's not good. I will tell her this as soon as I have a chance.*

"But that is not what I am asking about," repeats the mother. "I am asking why your God wanted to take my boy from me." Again, she sees her little Kostya as he was while he was alive. She hears his childish, melodious laughter ringing out like a little bell. "Why was he taken from me? If God could do this, then he is an evil god, and I do not need him or want to know him."

But what is this? Now Mary is not Mary but some strange new obscure being, and this being does not speak aloud, but somehow directly into the heart of the mother.

"You poor, blind, impertinent, and conceited creature," says this being. "You see your Kostya as he was a week ago, with his small, strong, flexible limbs, his long, curly hair, and his tender, naive, sensible speech. But has he always been like this? There was a time not long ago when you were happy he could say *Mama* and *Dada* and understand who is who. Before that, you admired how he stood up and, wobbling on his little legs, took his first steps. Even before that, you admired how he crawled around the room like a little animal. Before that, you were happy that he could hold up his bald little head that pulsated as he breathed. And even before that, you were glad that he took your breast and sucked it with his toothless gums. And before that, before the cord had even been cut, you were happy that he was all red, making his first cries in this world, trying the strength of his lungs. And even earlier, a year before that, where was he when he didn't even exist in this world? You think that you are stationary and that your life, and the lives of those you love, should continue to be as they are now. But you do not remain in the same place for even one minute. You are all flowing like a river, and like a stone, you are falling downwards to your death, which will come to all of you sooner or later. Don't you understand that if, from nothing, your son grew to become who he was, he would not have stopped changing for a single minute and would not have remained the same as he was when he died. Just as from nothing he became a suckling infant, from an infant he became a baby. From a baby he became a child. From a child he would have become a teenager, then a young man, then an adult, then an aging man, then a very old man. You do not know what he would have been if he had lived. But I know."

And then the mother sees a small, brightly lit room in the back of a restaurant. Her husband had once taken her to such a restaurant. Sitting at a table that holds the remains of supper is a rather fat, wrinkled old man with his nicely cut mustache curled upwards, an unpleasant old man trying to look younger. He sits deeply in a very soft sofa, and he peers with greedy, drunken eyes at a corrupt, heavily made-up woman baring her plump white neck, and his drunken tongue shouts and jokes rudely, cheered on by the laughter of another couple of the same sort.

"No, this is not true! This is not him, this is not my Kostya!" cries the mother, horrified by the terrible old man because there is, in fact, something in his look, in his lips, that reminds her of her Kostya.

It's all right. This is only a dream, she thinks. *The real Kostya is here.* And then she sees a naked, white Kostya with his plump little chest, sitting in the bathtub, laughing with her and splashing with his little feet. And she not only sees, but actually feels, how he grips her bare arm and kisses it, and then, not knowing what else to do, softly bites it.

Yes, this is my Kostya, and not that terrible old man, she says to herself. And with these words she wakes up, and with terror understands the reality she cannot escape.

She goes to the nursery. The servant has already washed and dressed Kostya. He has a high, thin, waxen nose. The small holes of his nostrils are still, and his soft hair is combed back from his forehead. He lies in state. There are candles and flowers around him, white and purple hyacinths. The nursemaid rises from the chair and, raising her eyebrows and pursing her lips, looks at the small, stony face of the child. Through the door opposite the mother, Mary enters, her face simple and kind, her eyes red from tears.

How is it that she just told me not to grieve, and yet she herself has been crying, thinks the mother. And then she glances at her dead son. She is immediately astonished by the terrible resemblance of this sweet small corpse to the face of the terrible old man she saw in her sleep. But she dispels this thought and, crossing herself, she touches her warm lips to the cold, waxen forehead. Then she kisses his cold, small hands, and the smell of hyacinths seems to tell her that he no longer exists, that he will never be here again. She cannot speak. She kisses his forehead again. And then she weeps for the first time. She cries not with hopeless tears, but with tears of joy and relief and release. She feels pain, but she does not resist it or complain. She knows now that what has happened should have happened, and therefore, it was good.

"It is a sin, dear mother, to cry," says the nurse, and coming to the small, dead body, she wipes away with her folded handkerchief the tears of the mother from Kostya's waxen forehead. "Your tears will burden his soul. All is well with him now. He is a sinless angel. And if he had lived, nobody knows what would have been."

"Yes, it is so. But it is so painful, so painful," says the mother.

THE
POOR
PEOPLE

The Poor People

In a fisherman's hut, a woman named Jeanne, the fisherman's wife, sits in front of the fire, mending sails. Outside, wind howls and whistles and huge waves pound the seashore. It is dark and cold outside, and the sea is stormy, but it is warm and cozy in the fisherman's hut. The earthen floor has been neatly swept, embers still burn in the oven, and the washed dishes on the shelf gleam. Behind a white curtain on the bed, five children sleep quietly, oblivious to the howling of the storm and the sea. Her husband, the fisherman, took his boat to sea early in the morning and has not yet come back.

Jeanne listens to the monotonous thud of the waves and the howling of the wind. She is afraid.

The old wooden clock, its voice hoarse, strikes ten o'clock, eleven o'clock. Her husband is not home yet. "He does not spare himself. He fishes even in stormy weather, and I sit from morning till night at my work," Jeanne says to herself. "And what else can we do? We can barely feed ourselves. The children do not even have proper shoes, they run barefoot in both summer and winter. And they do not eat white bread. It is a good thing that we at least have enough black rye bread to feed our children. And the only food they have besides bread is fish. Well, thank God, the children are healthy. We cannot complain." She listens again to the storm. "But where is he? Oh God, save him and have mercy on him!" she says, and crosses herself.

It is too late to go to bed. Jeanne gets up, covers her hair with a thick shawl, lights a lantern, and goes outside to see if the sea is less stormy, or the dawn is rising, or if perhaps she can see the lighthouse or maybe the returning boat of her husband. But she can see nothing in the sea. The wind tears away her shawl and rattles something against the door of her neighbor's hut. Now Jeanne remembers that, earlier, she had intended to pay a visit to her sick neighbor next door. *There is no one to look after her,* Jeanne thinks as she knocks at the door. She listens. No one answers.

It is hard for a widow to make ends meet, thinks Jeanne, standing at the door. *Even though she does not have many children, only two, it has still been hard for her, especially since she fell ill. Oh, it is hard to be a widow. I'll go in and see her.*

Jeanne knocks again and again, but nobody answers. "Hey, neighbor!" Jeanne calls. *Maybe something has happened,* she thinks as she pushes open the door.

It is damp and cold in the hut. She holds up the lantern to see where the sick woman is. The first thing she notices is the bed, just in front of the door, and on the bed she sees her neighbor, lying so quiet and motionless, as only dead people can lie. Jeanne moves her lantern even closer. Yes, it is her. Her head tilts backwards, and on the cold blue face is the quiet expression of death. Her pale dead hand hangs from the straw-covered bed, as if she had tried to get hold of something during her last moment.

And here, in a cradle not far from the bed of the mother, are two small children with curly heads and plump cheeks. Covered with an old dress, they sleep twisted together, with their small blond heads pressed close. Maybe before she died their mother managed to cover their legs with her warm shawl and wrap them with her dress. Their breathing is quiet and even. They sleep sweetly and soundly.

Jeanne takes the cradle with the children and, covering it with her own shawl, brings it home. Her heart is beating loudly. She does not know why she has done this, but she knows that she could not have done anything else.

In her home, she takes the children, who have not awakened, puts them into the bed with her own children, and quickly pulls the curtain. She is pale and excited, tortured by her conscience. *What will he say?* she asks herself. *This is no laughing matter. We have five children of our own, and more than enough to do for them. Is that him? No, it's still not him. Why did I take them? He'll beat me for it. It would serve me right, I deserve it. There he is! No . . . well, it's better that way.*

The door creaks, as if somebody has entered. Jeanne rises quickly from her chair.

No, again there is no one there. Oh, God, why did I do this? And how will I look him in the eyes? Jeanne wonders, and sits at the edge of the bed quietly for a long time.

The rain has stopped. The dawn is rising, but the wind is still howling as it has the whole night.

Suddenly, the door opens, and a rush of fresh sea air pushes into the room. A tall, dark-skinned fisherman enters, pulling his wet, torn nets with him. "Here I am, Jeanne," he says.

"Oh, it's you," says Jeanne, frozen in her place, without looking at him.

"What a night we have had! Terrible!"

"Yes, yes, the weather was horrible. And how was your fishing?"

"Rotten, completely rotten. I caught nothing. I only tore my net. Too bad, the weather we are having! I don't think I can remember a night this terrible for a long time. Thank God I came home alive! So what did you do here while I was gone?"

The fisherman drags his net into the room and sits near the stove.

"Well," Jeanne replies, "I sat, I did some needlework. The wind howled, and I was afraid for you."

"Yes, yes, the weather was terrible, but what can we do?" her husband mutters.

They were quiet for a while.

"You know," says Jeanne, "our neighbor, Simone, has died."

"What?"

"I don't know when. Maybe even yesterday. Imagine how hard it must have been for her, to die and leave behind her children. How her heart must have ached for them! She had two—they are so small. One can't talk yet and the other has just started to crawl."

Jeanne grows silent. The fisherman frowns and his face becomes serious and worried.

"Well," he says, scratching the back of his head. "But what can we do? We have to take them. Otherwise, when they awaken, they will find themselves with the body of a dead woman. Well, we will survive somehow. Hurry and get them."

But Jeanne does not move from her place.

"What's wrong with you? Don't you want to? What's happened, Jeanne?"

"Here they are," says Jeanne, and she pulls the curtain aside.

A Coffeehouse
in the
City of Surat

A Coffeehouse in the City of Surat

In the Indian city of Surat there was a coffeehouse. People from many lands, travelers and foreigners, came there for conversation.

Once, a Persian religious scholar came to this coffeehouse. All of his life, he had studied the essence of God, and he had read and written many books on the subject. He thought and read and wrote about God until everything got mixed up in his head, and he reached the point that he stopped believing in God.

When the Persian king discovered this, he exiled the scholar from his kingdom.

The poor scholar became confused, and instead of perceiving that he had lost his own mind, he thought that the divine mind which governs this world was lost.

This scholar had a slave, an African man who followed him everywhere. When the scholar went into the coffeehouse, the African man stayed outside, sitting on a stone in the sunshine, swatting at the summer flies. The scholar reclined on a sofa inside the coffeehouse and asked for a serving of opium. When he had drunk it, he felt better, and he asked his slave a question. "Hey, slave," said the scholar, "tell me, what do you think: Is there a god or not?"

"Certainly there is a god!" the slave answered, and he pulled a small wooden idol out of his belt. "Here, this is the god who has preserved me since I was born into this world. This god is made from a branch of the most holy of trees, which is worshiped by everyone in my country."

The people sitting in the coffeehouse listened to this conversation and were surprised, both by the question of the master and, even more so, by the answer of the slave.

Then one of the Indian Brahmins who heard the slave's reply addressed him. "You poor and foolish man—do you really think that god can be carried in a man's belt? There is only one god, and his name is Brahma. Brahma is bigger than the whole world, because he created the world. Brahma is the only god, and he is great, and all the temples along the river Ganges are dedicated to him. He is the god whom all Brahmin priests serve. These priests know the only real and true god. There have been Brahmin priests for more than 120,000 years, and no matter how many changes take place in this world, the Brahmin priesthood will be here forever because Brahma, the one true god, protects us."

The Brahmin priest said this to convince all present, but a Jewish moneychanger who was there disagreed with him. "No," he said, "the temple of the real God is not in India. And God does not protect the Brahmin caste! The true God is not the god of the Brahmins but the God of Abraham, Isaac, and Jacob. And this God protects only his people, Israel. From the beginning of the world, God has loved, and still loves, our people alone. And if now our people are scattered all over the world, this is only a trial for us. God, as he has promised, will gather all his people in Jerusalem to restore that ancient wonder, the temple of Jerusalem, and he will establish the king of Israel above all other nations."

At this point the Jewish man began to cry. He wanted to continue, but he was interrupted by an Italian.

"You do not tell the whole truth," said the Italian to the Jew. "You describe God as unjust. God cannot love one nation more than another. To the contrary, even if he once protected Israel, more than 1800 years have passed since God became furious at this people, and as a sign of his wrath scattered the Israelite people all over the earth. Now the Jewish faith is not being spread, but survives in only a few places. God does not show preference for any particular nation, but he calls all who want to be saved into membership in the Roman Catholic Church, outside of which there is no salvation."

When he heard the words of the Italian, a Protestant pastor who was present turned pale, and he replied, "How can you claim that salvation is possible only though your church? You should know that, according to the New Testament, those who will be saved are only those who serve God in spirit and in truth, according to Jesus' commandment."

Then a Turkish customs officer from the city of Surat, who had been smoking his pipe with an important air, interrupted the conversation and addressed both Christians. "Your confidence in the truth of your Roman church is unfounded. Your religion was replaced about six hundred years ago by the genuinely true religion of Mohammed. As you can see for yourself, the true faith of Mohammed is spreading across Europe, Africa, Asia, and even into enlightened China. You yourselves admit that the Jews were rejected by God, and as proof of this, you said that the Jewish people are oppressed and that their numbers are decreasing. Accordingly, you should accept the truth of the religion of Mohammed, because it is at the height of its glory and is spreading further and further around the world. Only those who believe in the teaching of Mohammed, God's last prophet, will be saved. And only those who are the followers of Oman and not Ali will be saved, because the followers of Ali are unfaithful."

At this point, the Persian religious scholar, who belonged to Ali's sect, wanted to object, but a great argument broke out among the foreigners throughout the coffeehouse, who all belonged to different religions and faiths. There were Christians from Abyssinia, Lamas from India, Ishmaelites, and even fire-worshipers. Everyone argued about the essence of God and the proper way to praise and worship him. Everyone said that only in his own country did people know the true God and the way to worship him correctly.

All the people in the coffeehouse were arguing loudly. Only a Chinese man, a student of Confucius, sat quietly in the corner of the coffeehouse, declining to participate in the discussion. He drank his tea, listened to what the others said, but himself remained silent.

The Turk, who noticed him, addressed him. "Please take my side, dear Chinaman. You sit here quietly, but I know that you can say something in my favor, for in China, in your country, many different religions are being introduced and practiced. Your merchants told me that Chinese of different faiths consider the Muslim religion to be the best, and they accept it readily. So please tell me what you think of the only true God and of his prophet."

"Yes, yes, tell us your opinion!" all the others insisted.

The Confucian closed his eyes for a moment, then opened them, spread his hands from the wide sleeves of his gown, crossed them on his breast, and spoke in a quiet, low voice.

❧

"Gentlemen," he said, "it seems to me that, most of the time, people's pride and selfishness interfere with their agreement on questions of faith. If you will be so kind as to listen to me, I will gladly illustrate this opinion with an example.

"I traveled from China to Surat on a British steamship sailing around the world. On the way, we stopped at a harbor on the eastern side of the island of Sumatra to get drinking water. By noon, we had disembarked, and we sat on the seashore under the shadows of the coconut trees, not far from the local village. Several people from different countries were in our company.

"While we sat there, a blind man approached us.

"This man had become blind, as we later discovered, because he had stared stubbornly at the sun for a very long time in order to understand its essence. He wanted to know this so that he could become the master of sunlight.

"He tried again and again, employing every science, to trap a few rays of sunlight and put them into a bottle. His many attempts to do this, while he looked at the sun, were unsuccessful, and in the end his eyes were burned and he became blind.

"Then he reasoned to himself: 'The light is not a liquid; otherwise, if it were liquid, it could flow from one vessel to another and it would have waves and vibrations caused by the wind, as water has. Sunlight is not a fire, because if it were a fire, it could be extinguished by water. Sunlight is not a spirit because it can be observed, and yet it is not a body because one cannot move it from one place to another. Therefore, since sunlight is neither liquid, nor fire, nor spirit, nor body, sunlight is—nothing.'

"Thus the man lost both his intellect and his eyesight while arriving at these conclusions and staring intently at the sun. By the time he was completely blind, he had also become completely assured that the sun did not exist.

"This was the blind man who approached us as we were sitting on the beach. He was accompanied by his slave. The slave settled his master under the shadow of a coconut tree, picked up a coconut from the ground, and began to make a lamp from it. First he made a wick from the fiber of the nut, then he poured some coconut oil inside the shell and thus made a lantern. While the slave was making his lamp, the blind man poked him and said, 'So, slave, did I explain that there is no sun? You see, it's very dark now. So then, what is the sun?'

"'I don't know what the sun is, and I don't care. But I know about light. Here, I have made a lamp for myself. I will have some light at night, and I will be able to serve you, and to find everything in my hut.' The servant held up the coconut-shell lamp in his hand and said, 'This is my sunshine.'

"There was a lame man on the beach, supporting himself with crutches. He listened to this and laughed at the blind one. 'Perhaps you've been blind from birth, and don't know what sunshine is. But I can tell you: The sun is a ball of fire, and every morning this ball rises up from the sea, and at night it sets behind the mountains of our island. We can see this, and you could too, if only you had eyesight.'

"A fisherman who was sitting there among us said to the lame man, 'Probably you have never left this island in your lifetime. If you were not lame, you could travel across the sea, and then you would notice that the sun does not set behind the mountains of your island. As it rises from the sea, so it sets into the sea in the evening. And I know this for certain because I see it every day with my own eyes.'

"The Indian man sitting with us heard this and said, 'I am surprised that a clever person could say such a stupid thing. How is it possible that a ball of fire could descend into the water and the fire not be extinguished? The sun is not a ball of fire, it is a deity, and this deity is called Diva. This deity travels in a chariot across the sky around the golden mountain of Meruva. Sometimes, two evil snakes named Raghu and Ketu attack Diva and swallow it, and then it becomes dark, but our priests pray for the deity to be freed, and it becomes free. Only an ignorant person like you, who has never traveled further than your island, could imagine that the sun shines only here.'

"Then the owner of an Egyptian vessel began to speak. 'No,' he said, 'this is not true. The sun is not a deity that revolves only around India and its golden mountain. I have crossed the Black Sea, and visited the shores of Arabia; I have been to the island of Madagascar and also to the Philippines. The sun shines over all lands, not only India. Nor does it revolve around one mountain, but it rises up from behind the Japanese islands. Those islands are called *Ja-Pan*, which means in their language, "the birth of the sun." And then it goes down far, far away in the West, behind the islands of England. I know this myself, because I have seen much and heard much from my grandfather. My grandfather made voyages to the very ends of the earth.'

"He started to add something else, but the British sailor from our ship interrupted him. 'There is no country besides England,' he said, 'where people would know better how the sun moves across the sky. The sun, as all Englishmen know, does not rise anywhere or set anywhere. It constantly revolves around the earth. We know this because we have just traveled around the world ourselves, and we did not run across the sun on our way. In all places, just like here, it appears in the morning and disappears at night.'

"The British sailor took a stick, drew a circle on the sand, and started explaining how the sun moves around the earth. But, afraid that his explanation was not sufficient, he looked up at the skipper of his ship and said, 'He is better educated than I, and he can tell you more about it.'

"The skipper was a clever man, and he had listened to the conversation silently until now. But now that all had turned their attention to him, he began to speak. 'You are all deceiving each other, and you are all deceived. The sun does not move around the earth; rather, the earth moves around the sun. In addition, the earth rotates on its own axis, turning each place—including Japan, the Philippines, and Sumatra, where we are at present, and Europe, and Africa, and Asia, and all other countries—toward the sun every twenty-four hours. The sun gives light not only for one mountain, or one island, or one sea, and not even for one earth, but for many other planets as well. You would understand all this if you would look up in the sky, and not under your feet, and if you would admit that the sun doesn't shine exclusively in your country.'

"These were the words of the wise skipper who had been around the world many times, who had visited many countries, and who had studied the sky for a long time."

"Yes, all these errors and differences in faith come from pride," continued the Chinese Confucian. "And the errors heard in the discussion about the sun were repeated in your discussion of the notion of God. Every person wanted to have his own god, or at least a god for his homeland. Every nation wanted to define its own borders and limits for that which cannot be embraced or understood, even by the whole world.

"And tell me now, whose temple can compare with that which was created by God himself when he wanted to unite all people into one faith? All human temples are copies of this temple—that is, the world created by God. All temples have domes and ceilings, all temples have lanterns, icons, images, inscriptions, books of laws, sacrifices, altars, and priests. Which temple has a bath as great as the world's oceans, or a dome as high as the heavenly dome, or lanterns like the sun, moon, and stars; or images such as people living together, loving and helping each other? Are there any mere inscriptions about the love of God that are more easily understood than the blessings God gives us for our happiness? Where is the book of law more easily understood than the law of love, which is written on our hearts? Where are the sacrifices equal to the ones people give every day to those they love? Where is the altar that compares with the heart of a kind person in which God himself receives the sacrifice?

"The more one tries to understand God, the closer one will come to him, reflecting God's goodness, mercy, and love to everyone.

"Let him who sees the whole light of the sun that fills the world not despise the superstitious man who sees only one ray of this very same sun in his idol. Let him also not despise the unbeliever, who is blind and cannot see any light at all."

When the Chinese man had said this, all the people in the coffeehouse ceased their arguments about whose religion was the best.

KORNEI
VASILIEV

Kornei Vasiliev

Kornei Vasiliev was fifty-four years old when he visited his village for the last time. There was not a single gray hair on his thick, curly head, and one could see only a few gray hairs in his dark beard. His face was shiny and rosy, the back of his neck was wide and firm, and his strong body was covered with a layer of fat because of his comfortable city life.

About twenty years before, he had retired from the army and returned home with money. First, he opened his own retail shop. Then he gave up the retail business to become a cattle wholesaler. He would go to the Cherkassy region in the south of Russia to buy his "merchandise," as he called it, and then bring it to Moscow.

In his iron-roofed brick house in the village of Gayee lived his old mother; his wife and two children (a girl and a boy); his orphan nephew, who was a mute fifteen-year-old youth; and a servant. Kornei had been married twice. His first wife had been a weak, sickly woman who died childless. Then, when he was already an older widower, he married for the second time. His new wife was a healthy, beautiful woman, the daughter of a poor widow from a neighboring village. Both of his children were born to his second wife.

Kornei had so profitably sold the last of his "merchandise" in Moscow that he had made about three thousand rubles. He had learned from one of his friends that, not far from his village, one could make a great profit by buying forest land from a landlord who had gone bankrupt. So Kornei decided to trade in real estate and timber. He had gained some knowledge of this before his army service, when he had been a sales manager's assistant, selling wood.

At the railway station, not far from the village of Gayee, Kornei met his neighbor, Kuzma, a poor farmer who lived in Gayee. He used to drive his horse cart from Gayee to meet every arriving train and give a ride to the people going into the village. The cart was drawn by two very weak, hairy, small horses. Kuzma was a poor man and hated all rich people, especially the rich Kornei, whom he called Korniushka.

Kornei was wearing two warm coats, a half-length fur coat and a long winter sheepskin coat, and carried a small suitcase in his hand. With his belly bulging beneath his trousers, he stepped onto the platform and stood there, panting and looking around. It was morning. The weather was calm and cloudy with a light frost.

"Haven't found a fare, Uncle Kuzma? Will you give me a ride home?"

"Certainly I will. Give me a ruble."

"Seventy kopecks is enough."

"Well, you have such a big belly, and you want to steal thirty kopecks from a poor man?"

"Let's go. Are you coming, or what?" said Kornei.

Then Kornei put his case in the back of the sledges, along with some of the rest of his baggage, and sat comfortably on the back seat. Kuzma sat in the front seat. "All right, let's go." They drove out of the potholes at the station onto a smooth road. "So, how are you doing? What's going on? I don't mean at our place, but at your place, in the village?"

"There is little good to say."

"Why is that? Is my old mother alive?"

"Yes, your old mother is alive. She went to church recently, and I saw her there. Your mother is alive. And your young lady is alive as well. What could happen to her? She just hired a new worker." And Kuzma laughed strangely, or so it seemed to Kornei.

"What kind of worker? Was it Peter, or whom?"

"Peter got sick. She took on Evstignei, the blond fellow from the Kamenka village," said Kuzma. "From her old village, that is."

"Oh, really?" asked Kornei.

Some time before, when Kornei had been about to marry Marfa, some old women in the village had spread rumors about Evstignei.

"That's how it goes, Kornei Vasilich," said Kuzma. "Nowadays women have too much freedom."

"Well, you are right about that," said Kornei. "And your old horse has turned gray," he said, wanting to change the subject.

"I am not young anymore myself, and my horse is like her master," answered Kuzma, and he whipped his hairy old gelding.

Halfway between the village and the railway station, there was an inn with a tavern. Kornei asked to stop there and got down from the cart. Kuzma moved his horses to the empty furrow, fixed the reins without looking at Kornei, and waited to see if he would ask him inside.

"Come on in, Uncle Kuzma," said Kornei, going up the porch. "Let's have a shot of vodka."

"Well, all right," said Kuzma, pretending to be in no hurry.

Kornei asked for a bottle of vodka and treated Kuzma. Kuzma had not eaten since the morning, and soon he felt a little drunk. Soon the drink loosened his tongue, and he bowed his head closer to Kornei and told him in a whisper of the gossip that was circulating in the village. People were saying that Marfa, Kornei's wife, had hired her former lover as a household worker and was living with him.

"Well, I don't care much. It is all the same to me. But I feel sorry for you," said the drunk Kuzma. "Only it's not good that people are laughing. It's obvious she is not afraid of sin. Well, you just wait a little, I told them. Give it some time, he'll be back, the husband. He will return. So there you are, my friend, Kornei Vasilievich."

Kornei listened quietly to what Kuzma told him, and his thick eyebrows moved lower and lower above his dark eyes, which were shining like two pieces of coal. "So, will you buy me a drink now?" Kornei said when the bottle was empty. "If not, then let us go."

Kornei paid the owner of the tavern, and they went out.

They arrived home as it was getting dark. The first person Kornei met was the very Evstignei the Blond, whom he hadn't been able to get out of his mind the whole way home. Kornei said hello to him. Seeing the thin, tow-haired face of Evstignei, who was hurrying about his work, Kornei shook his head in bewilderment.

Maybe he lied to me, the old fool, he said, thinking about what Kuzma had told him. *But you never know. Well, I will find out everything.*

Kuzma stood by his horse and winked at Evstignei.

"So, you live here, at our place?" asked Kornei.

"Well, I have to work somewhere," said Evstignei.

"Has the room been heated up?"

"Yes. And Matveevna, the old woman, is inside," answered Evstignei.

Kornei went up onto the porch. Marfa heard the voices and came out. Seeing her husband, she blushed, and then hastily and especially tenderly greeted him. "We have been waiting for you, and we almost stopped expecting you," she said, following Kornei inside to the living room.

"And so—how have you been without me?"

"Well, life goes on as it always has," she said. Picking up her two-year-old daughter, who was tugging on her skirt and asking for some milk to drink, Marfa strode resolutely into the entrance hall.

Kornei's mother, with the same dark eyes as Kornei, came into the living room, hardly moving her feet in her winter boots.

"Thank you for coming to visit us," she said, nodding her trembling head in a greeting.

Kornei told his mother why he had come and how his business was, and then he remembered about Kuzma and went out to pay him his money. As soon as he opened the door into the entrance hall, he saw Marfa and Evstignei. They stood very close to each other, and she was saying something to him. As soon as Kornei appeared, Evstignei quickly went outside, and Marfa began fixing the samovar.

Kornei silently passed her as she stood bent over the pot. He picked up the suitcases he had brought with him, and asked Kuzma into the living room for a cup of tea. Before they had tea, Kornei gave out the gifts he brought his family from Moscow: a big woolen shawl for his mother, a children's picture book for his son, Fyodor, a vest for his mute nephew, and a piece of fine cotton cloth for a dress for his wife.

While they drank tea, Kornei sat at the table, looking very downcast and depressed. Only occasionally did he smile reluctantly and look up, watching the mute man who entertained everyone with his joy. His new vest made him happy, and he admired it, put it down on the table, wrapped it up, unwrapped it, and then put it on and kissed his own hand, looking at Kornei and smiling.

After tea and supper, Kornei went into the bedroom where he slept with his wife Marfa and small daughter. Marfa remained in the living room to wash up the dishes. Kornei sat alone at the table, resting on his forearms and waiting, becoming more and more angry at his wife. He took down an abacus from the wall, pulled out a notebook from his pocket, and to distract himself, began to reckon his accounts, looking at the door from time to time and listening to the voices in the living room.

He heard the outside door to their home open several times, and someone came into their entrance hall, but it was not her. At last he heard her steps. The door opened and she came in, a beautiful woman with rosy cheeks, her head covered with a red kerchief, holding their small daughter in her arms.

"I guess you are tired after your long trip," she said, as if she did not notice that he looked so gloomy.

Kornei looked up at her and then continued with his accounting, even though everything had already been accounted for.

"Well, it's already late," she said, and setting the small girl down, went behind the screen in the corner of the bedroom.

He heard her making up their daughter's bed and putting her into it.

People are laughing at me, he thought, remembering Kuzma's words. *Wait, wait a little.* He tried to control his breathing. He stood slowly, put the little pencil stub into his breast pocket, hung his abacus on a nail in the wall, and took off his coat. He came to the screen and looked at his wife's face as, before the icons, she prayed to God. She stood facing the icons and praying. He stopped and waited. She crossed herself and bowed for a long time, whispering her prayers. It seemed to Kornei that she recited all the prayers she knew and repeated them several times on purpose, to take a longer time. At the end she bowed very low to the ground, straightened, whispered a few last words of prayer, and turned to him.

"Agashka is already sleeping," she said, pointing toward their daughter. Smiling, she sat on her bed, which creaked under her weight.

"Has Evstignei lived here for long?" he asked, coming closer to her.

Quietly, she brought her thick plait of hair over her shoulder to her breast and started unbraiding it with quick movements of her fingers. She looked directly at him, and her eyes were laughing at him.

"Evstignei? I don't know—maybe two or three weeks."

"Do you live with him?" Kornei asked her.

She let the plait fall from her hand, but immediately took up her thick stiff hair and started to braid it again.

"What things people can think up! That I live with Evstignei?" she said, saying the name *Evstignei* especially loudly. "What will they think up next?"

"Tell me, is it true or not?" asked Kornei, and he clenched his strong hands into fists in his pockets.

"Stop talking about such stupid things. Can I take your boots off?"

"I am asking you," he repeated.

"Well, what are you saying? That I am tempted by Evstignei? And who lied to you about this?"

"What were you talking to him about, just now in the entrance hall?"

"What did I talk to him about? I asked him to fix a barrel hoop, and that's it. Why are you badgering me?"

"I am ordering you—tell me the truth. Otherwise I will kill you." He grabbed her by the hair.

Grimacing with pain, she managed to pull her hair from his hands. "All you can do is to fight. What good did I ever see in you? Living such a life, one might do anything."

"What 'anything' did you do?" he said, moving closer to her.

"Why did you pull me by the hair? Now my hair is hanging in tangles. What did you pester me for? And it is true that—" She did not get the chance to finish her speech.

He grasped her hand, yanked her from the bed, and began beating her with great force on her head, her sides, her breasts. The more he beat her, the more angry he became. She cried, trying to defend herself, trying to escape, but he would not let her go. Their daughter woke up and ran to her mother. "Mommy!" she cried.

Kornei grabbed the little girl by the hand, tore her away from her mother, and threw her into the corner like a kitten. The girl screamed and then became completely quiet for quite a long moment.

"You criminal! You have killed your child!" cried Marfa, trying to get closer to her daughter. But Kornei grabbed her again and struck her breast so hard that she fell down and stopped yelling. Only the little girl cried desperately, without taking a breath.

The old woman, his mother, her gray hair loose and her head shaking from side to side, came into the small room. Without looking at either Kornei or Marfa, she went to her granddaughter, whose face was covered with tears of despair, and picked her up.

Kornei stood breathing heavily, looking around him as if he could not understand where he was or who was with him.

Marfa raised her head, and, moaning, wiped her still-bleeding face with her undershirt. "You hateful scoundrel! You villain! Yes, I have been living with Evstignei. Go ahead, beat me to death. And Agashka is not your daughter; she is his," she said quickly, and shielded her face with her elbow, waiting for another blow.

But it was as if Kornei did not understand. He continued breathing heavily, looking around him.

"Look what you did to the little girl! You broke her arm!" said his old mother, indicating the dislocated arm of the baby, who cried unceasingly. Kornei turned and, without saying a word, went out through the entrance hall onto the porch.

Outside, it was still gloomy and frosty. Occasional snowflakes fell onto his burning cheeks and forehead. He sat down on the stairs, took handfuls of snow from the rails, and started eating it. From behind the door came the sounds of Marfa moaning and the incessant crying of the little girl. The door in the entrance hall opened, and he heard his mother and the little girl leave the bedroom and go through the hall to the big house. He stood and went back into the bedroom. A lamp on the table lit the room dimly. From behind the curtain, Marfa's moans grew louder as he entered. He dressed silently, took his case from behind the bed, put his belongings into it, and closed it, binding it with a length of rope.

"Why did you kill me? Why? What did I do to you?" said Marfa in a pitiful voice.

Kornei picked up his case without answering her and went to the door.

"You are a criminal, a prisoner! Just you wait! Do you think I won't bring charges against you?" she said in a different, hostile voice.

Without answering her, Kornei pushed open the door of his house with his foot, went out, and then shut it behind him, banging it so loudly that the walls of his house trembled.

Then Kornei went into the big adjoining house, woke up the mute boy, and ordered him to harness the horse. The half-asleep mute did not understand him at first, looking with surprise at his uncle, questioning him with his eyes, and combing his hair with both his hands. When at last he understood what Kornei wanted from him, he jumped up, put on his winter boots and his old shabby sheepskin coat, took a lantern, and went outside.

Dawn was glowing as Kornei joined the mute man, who sat in a small sledge outside the gates, and traveled back along the same route by which he had arrived the night before with Kuzma.

He arrived at the railway station five minutes before the train's departure. The mute man watched as Kornei bought a ticket, picked up his suitcase, found a seat in the railway carriage, and nodded his head. Then the railway car rolled out of sight.

Marfa's face was beaten badly. Two of her ribs were broken, and her head was injured. But being a strong and healthy young woman, she recovered. In half a year, there were no signs of the beating. But the little girl's arm was deformed for the rest of her life. Two bones of her forearm had been broken, and her arm was left crooked.

No one heard anything about Kornei after he left home, not even whether he was alive or dead.

II

Seventeen years had passed. It was late fall. The sun was lowering over the horizon, and it was getting dark at only four o'clock. The herd of cattle from Andreevka was going home for the night. The cowherd brought the cattle to the village, finished his hours, and left; then, women and children drove the herd home.

The herd had just left the harvested barley field and was moving along the local road, filling the air with their unceasing mooing and bleating as they approached the village. The road was unpaved and dirty, covered with cattletracks and dark mud, cut by the wheels of carts. A tall old man walked ahead of the herd, in its path. His beard and curly hair were gray; only his thick eyebrows were black. He wore a heavily mended cotton coat wet with rain and a big hat, and he bore a leather bag on his bent shoulders. He made his way through the mud in his wet, worn-out, Ukrainian leather boots, supporting every other step with a walking stick of oak. When the herd caught up with him, he stopped and leaned on his oaken stick. A young woman, her head covered with a piece of cloth, the end of her skirt tucked into her belt, wearing men's boots, was coming along the road, running with small steps from one side of the road to another, urging those sheep and pigs lagging behind. When she reached the old man, she stopped and looked at him.

"How are you, old man?" she said, her young voice pleasant and tender.

"Hello, my dear," the old man said.

"Are you planning to spend the night here?"

"Probably so. I'm tired," the old man said hoarsely.

"Well, old man, you don't have to go to the mayor's house," the young woman said tenderly. "Come straight to our place, the third hut from the end. My mother-in-law lets pilgrims spend the night for free."

"The third hut. You're a Zinoviev, aren't you?" the old man said, raising his eyebrows meaningfully.

"How do you know?"

"I've been here before."

"Hey, Fediushka, you aren't paying attention to the cattle—the lame one is lagging far behind!" the young woman cried, pointing at a three-legged sheep; then she waved a stick in the air with her right hand, and holding her other hand in an awkward way as she fixed the piece of cloth on her head, she ran back to get the wet lame black sheep.

The old man was Kornei. And the young woman was the same Agashka whose arm he had broken seventeen years before. She had married a man from a rich family in the village of Andreevka, four versts from Gayee.

III

Kornei Vasiliev had become a completely different man. He had once been a strong, rich, proud man—now he had become an old beggar with nothing but shabby clothes on his back, a soldier's ID, and two shirts in his bag. This change had been so gradual that he could not tell exactly when it had started and how it had happened. There was only one thing he knew with confidence: the reason for all his misfortunes was his evil wife. It was strange and painful for him to remember what he had been before. And when he did remember, he recalled with hatred the woman who, he believed, was the reason for all the misfortunes that had befallen him for the past seventeen years.

On the night he had beaten his wife, he had gone to see the landlord who was selling his forest. But Kornei Vasiliev could not buy the forest. It was already sold, so he returned to Moscow and started drinking. He had drunk before, but this time he drank for two weeks without interruption. When he came to his senses, he went south to buy cattle. He did not strike a good bargain, and lost money. He went south a second time, but the second deal did not work out either. A year later, he had only twenty-five rubles left from the three thousand he had started with, and he had to look for a job. He had always drunk from time to time, but now he did it more and more often.

First he worked as a steward for a big cattle dealer, but while on the job, he started drinking again, and the owner fired him. Through friends, he found a job with a wine dealer, but he did not last long there either; he fouled up the bookkeeping and was fired. He was ashamed to go home, and also filled with anger. *They will manage without me. Maybe the boy isn't mine either,* he thought.

Life got worse and worse. He could not live without his wine. He applied for a new job, this time not as a steward but as a cattle driver, but he could not get hired even for that.

The more difficult his life became, the more he accused her and the more he burned with anger at her.

Kornei's last job had been as a cattle driver for a man he didn't know. The herd fell ill. Kornei was not to blame, but the owner became angry, and he fired both Kornei and the steward. Because there was no other place to look for a job, Kornei decided to become a pilgrim. He made himself good boots and a backpack; he took some tea, sugar, and eight rubles and went to Kiev. He did not like it there, so he left for New Athon in the Caucasus. Before he made it there, he caught a fever. Suddenly he felt weak. He had very little money left, only one ruble and seventy kopecks, and he had no friends. He decided to go back home to his son. *Maybe she has died already, my evil woman,* he thought. *And if she is alive, I will tell her everything—she should know, the bitch, what she has done to my life,* he thought, and started for home.

He was feverish every other day. He became weaker, and could not walk more than ten or fifteen versts a day. About two hundred versts from home, he ran out of money, and still he went on, asking the villagers for food and the mayors of the villages for shelter in the name of Christ. *You can rejoice over what you have brought me to,* he thought about his wife, and, out of habit, his old and weak hands clenched into fists. But there was nobody to beat, and anyway he had no strength left in his hands.

It took him two weeks to walk those two hundred versts, and, ill and weak, he had come to this place, four versts from home, where he had met Agashka. He did not recognize her, and she did not recognize him, even though she was the girl (thought to be his daughter, although she was not really) whose hand he had broken.

IV

He did exactly as Agashka had told him. When he came to the Zinoviev house, he asked to spend the night. They let him in.

When he came into the house, he crossed himself before the icons, as he always did, and greeted the owners.

"You must be cold, old man! Come here, come here, closer to the stove," said the cheerful, wrinkled old woman, widow of the former owner, as she set the table.

Agashka's husband, a rather young man, was sitting at the table fixing a lamp. "Well, you are soaked to the bone, old man!" he said. "That won't do. Please, dry yourself off—right over there."

Kornei took off his coat and his boots, hung his wet socks to dry, and climbed onto the bed over the stove.

Agashka came into the house, carrying a jar. She had already brought in the herd and taken care of the cattle. "Have you seen the old pilgrim?" she asked. "I told him to come to our house."

"Here he is," said the owner, indicating the bed where Kornei sat scratching his hairy bony legs.

They asked Kornei to join them for tea. He sat down at the end of the bench. They gave him a cup and a lump of sugar. Then they spoke about the weather and the harvest, which had not been good that year. The crops in the landlords' fields had not been gathered, and the grain had started to spoil. As soon as they tried to gather the harvest, it would start to rain again. The peasants had managed to gather their own grain, but the rich landlords did not care. And there were so many mice in the sheaves.

Kornei said that on his way, he had seen a whole field covered with sheaves. The young woman poured him a fifth cup of very weak, watery tea, and gave it to him.

"It's all right. Drink up, old man, and get well," she said when he tried to refuse.

"Why doesn't your hand work right?" he asked, taking the cup of hot tea carefully from her and raising his eyebrows.

"It was broken when she was young. It was her own father who wanted to kill her, our dear Agashka," said the talkative mother-in-law.

"Why?" Kornei asked. Then, looking at the face of the young woman, he suddenly remembered Evstignei the Blond with his light-blue eyes, and his hand holding the cup started to tremble so that he spilled half of his tea before he could put it on the table.

"There was a man here in Gayee—her father. His name was Kornei Vasiliev. He was a rich man. And he was a proud man, who was suspicious of his wife. He beat her up and crippled this girl."

Kornei kept silent, gazing steadily from beneath his raised eyebrows, looking in turn at the owner and at Agashka. "What did he do that for?" he asked, biting into his lump of sugar.

"Nobody knows why. People spread different rumors about us women, and you can't answer them all," the old woman said. "The trouble was over a workman she hired. He was a nice young man from our village. Then he died in their house."

"He died?" Kornei asked, coughing.

"He died a long time ago. Then we took this young woman from their family. We lived very well, and were the wealthiest in our village. While my husband was still alive."

"And what happened to the father?" Kornei asked.

"He probably died too. He just disappeared. It was over fifteen years ago."

"It cannot be more than that, because my mother told me that she had just weaned me from the breast when it happened."

"Tell me, how do you feel about that man—do you hate him for breaking your hand?" Kornei started to ask, but his voice broke off.

"He's *not* a stranger—but he is still my father, anyway. Well, old man, have some more tea and warm up. Can I pour you some?"

Kornei, weeping, did not answer.

"What's wrong, old man?"

"Nothing, nothing at all. Thank you, and Christ be with you."

Kornei gripped the edge of the bed with his trembling hands and, barefooted, climbed in.

"Look at him," the old woman said to her son, blinking at the old man.

V

The next day, Kornei woke up before anyone else. He climbed down from his bed over the stove, adjusted his clothes, put on his dried, stiff boots with some effort, and took up his backpack.

"Well, old man, won't you have breakfast with us?" the old woman asked.

"Thank you, in God's name. I have to go."

"Then at least take some of yesterday's scones. I will put some in your bag."

Kornei thanked her and said goodbye.

"Stop in again on your way back, if all goes well."

A thick autumn fog covered everything. But Kornei knew the road well—every turn, every descent and hill, every bush, every tree, every willow. He knew the forest on both sides of the road, even though, over the course of seventeen years, some old trees had been cut and replaced by young ones, and some young trees had become old.

The village of Gayee was much the same, although several new houses that weren't there before had appeared at the edge of the village. Formerly wooden houses had become brick. His brick house looked much the same as before, just older. The roof had not been painted for a long time, several bricks had fallen out at the corners, and the porch was leaning.

As he approached the house, a roan mare with her colt and a three-year-old stallion came out of the gate. The old roan looked exactly like the one Kornei had bought at the market a year before he left home. Perhaps, he thought, this was the horse that had been in the belly of its mother when he left his village. She had the same back, the same strong chest and hairy legs.

A dark-eyed boy in new peasant boots was driving the horses to water. *Maybe this is my grandson, Fyodor's son. He looks exactly like my son Fyodor, with the same black eyes,* Kornei thought.

The boy looked at the strange old man, then ran after the young stallion, who was playing in the road. A dog ran behind the boy, and it was as black as Volchok, Kornei's old dog.

Is it Volchok? No, it cannot be, he thought, remembering that Volchok would now be twenty years old.

Approaching the porch, he climbed the steps on which he had sat, a long time ago, eating snow from the rails. He opened the entrance door.

"Why do you enter the house without asking me?" asked a woman's voice from inside the house. He recognized her voice. And then there she was, a dry, skinny, wrinkled old woman who stuck out her face from behind the door. Kornei had expected to see the young, beautiful Marfa who had insulted him. He still hated that young woman and wanted to reproach her, but it was a strange old woman that he now saw in front of him.

"If you're begging for alms, you should ask through the window," her squeaky voice told him.

"I'm not here to beg."

"Then why are you here? What else do you want?"

Suddenly she stopped. And from the look on her face, he saw that she now recognized him. "Enough people, tramps like you, come by here every day. Go away, be off, and God be with you."

Kornei pressed his back against the wall, supporting himself with a stick, and looked at her intently. To his surprise, he found that, deep in his soul, he no longer felt the anger toward her that he had carried within him for so many years. Instead, a tender weakness suddenly embraced him.

"Marfa, we will all die soon."

"Go away, go away, and God be with you!" she said in an angry, malicious tone.

"You don't have anything else to say to me?"

"There is nothing more for me to say," she said. "Go away. God be with you. Be off! There are many people like you walking around here, tramps and bums."

With quick movements, she went back inside the house and slammed the door behind her.

"What are you scolding the old man for?" Kornei heard a man's voice, and then the door opened again, and a dark-haired peasant came out. He had an ax fixed on his belt. The man looked exactly as Kornei had forty years ago—only a bit thinner and shorter, but with the same dark, shining eyes.

This was his son, the same Fyodor who seventeen years before had received a children's picture book as a gift from his father. And it was Fyodor who now reproached his mother for not taking pity on a beggar.

A second man came out of the house. He too had an ax fixed to his belt. It was the mute nephew. Now he was a grown man with a thin beard and a wrinkled face, a rather skinny fellow with a long neck and resolute, piercing eyes. The two men had just had their breakfast and were going to the forest to chop wood.

"Wait a minute, old man," said Fyodor. Then, using a kind of sign language to communicate with the mute man, he indicated the old man, then the inside of the house, and then imitated the motion of cutting bread. Fyodor went outside, while the mute man returned to the house.

Still pressing himself against the wall and supporting himself with his stick, Kornei stood, head bowed. He felt very weak, and could hardly keep from sobbing.

The mute man emerged from the house again with a thick slice of freshly baked black rye bread. He crossed himself and gave it to Kornei. Kornei took the bread and also crossed himself. The mute man turned toward the entrance door, pressed both hands against his face for a second, and then acted as if he were going to spit—showing that he did not approve of the behavior of his aunt. He suddenly stopped, opened his mouth, and stared at Kornei, as if he recognized him. Kornei could not stop crying now; tears rolled down his face, and he wiped those tears and his eyes and nose and his gray beard with the flap of his caftan. Then he turned away from the mute man and went out onto the porch. He felt a strange bliss, a mixture of meekness, resignation, and humiliation; he felt it toward her, toward his son, toward all people, and this feeling of joy was tearing his soul apart.

Marfa watched from her window and breathed peacefully only when she saw that the old man had disappeared around the corner of the house. When she was sure that he had gone, she sat down and started her weaving. She worked the loom a dozen times, but her hands wouldn't cooperate, so she stopped and began to think. She knew that the man she had just seen was the same Kornei Vasiliev who had tortured and almost killed her—but who had also loved her, a long time ago. And she was frightened by what she had just done. She hadn't done what she should have. But how should she have behaved with him? He had not even told her that he was Kornei, and that he was returning home.

Then she returned to the shuttle and continued weaving until evening.

VI

Kornei returned with great difficulty to the neighboring village of Andreevka, and again he asked the Zinoviev family if he could spend the night in their home. They allowed him to come in.

"So, old man, you could go no further?"

"No. I became too weak. I think I should return. May I spend the night here?"

"Well, you will not make a hole in our bed if you spend the night. I am joking, of course. Come in and dry off near the stove."

The whole night through, Kornei suffered from a fever. In the morning he lost consciousness, and when he came to himself, all the people in the family had gone to work, leaving only Agashka in the house to take care of the household. He lay on top of the bed on a dry caftan the old woman had put there. Agashka pulled freshly baked bread from the oven.

"Dear girl," he addressed her, in a quiet, weak voice, "please come closer to me."

"Just a second, old man," she said, pulling out a loaf of bread. "Would you like something to drink? Some kvass?"

He did not answer.

When she had pulled out the last loaf of bread, she brought him a dipper of kvass. He did not turn toward her and did not drink, but began to speak to her as he lay there, looking at the ceiling. "Agashka," he said in a quiet voice, "my time has come. I want to die. So please forgive me, for the sake of Christ."

"God will forgive you. You have done nothing bad to me."

He was quiet for a while.

"Now, dear girl, go to your mother and speak to her. Tell her that the pilgrim . . . tell her that yesterday's pilgrim . . . tell her . . ." He began sobbing.

"Have you visited my family?"

"Yes, I have. I was there yesterday. Tell her that the pilgrim . . . the pilgrim . . ." Again he was stopped by his sobbing, and when he at last collected himself, he said, "I came to her to say goodbye." He began fumbling for something near his chest.

"I will tell her this, old man. Do not worry. What are you looking for?" said Agashka.

The old man, without answering, frowned, pulled out a paper with his thin hairy hand, and gave it to her.

"Give this to those people who will ask. This is my military ID. Now, thank God, all my sins are forgiven." His face took on a solemn expression. His eyebrows lifted, his eyes became fixed on the ceiling, and he grew silent.

"A candle," he said, without moving his lips.

Agashka understood him. She took from under the icons the remains of a wax candle, lit it, and gave it to the old man. He pressed it with his thumb.

She turned to put his military papers into a chest in the corner, and when she returned to him, the candle fell from his hands, his eyes went blank, and he stopped breathing. Agashka crossed herself, blew out the candle, took a clean white towel, and covered his face.

❧

Throughout the night, Marfa could not sleep for thinking about Kornei. In the morning, she put on her winter coat, covered her head with a shawl, and went to find out where the old man had gone. She soon learned that he had gone to the Andreevka village. Taking a stick from the hedge, Marfa followed. The further she went, the more scared she felt. *We should forgive each other. We should bring him home, and all our sins will be forgiven. Let him at least die at home, with his son,* she thought.

As Marfa approached her daughter's house, she saw a big crowd of people at the door. Some were standing in the entrance hall; others stood in front of the windows. Everyone had already heard that the famous rich man, Kornei Vasiliev, whose name had been well known all over the neighborhood twenty years ago, had died as a poor pilgrim in his daughter's house. The house was full of people. Women were whispering, moaning, and sighing.

When Marfa came into the house, people moved to both sides to let her through, and under the icons she saw the dead body which had been washed, cleaned, and covered with a white cloth. Above him, Philip Kononych, the only man in the village who could read, acted as a deacon, and read the old Slavonic words of the psalter.

There was no one for her to forgive and no one to ask forgiveness from. And from Kornei's stern, beautiful old face, it was impossible to tell whether he forgave her or was still angry.

A Grain
of Rye
the Size of a
Chicken Egg

A Grain of Rye the Size of a Chicken Egg

Once upon a time, some boys found an object the size of a chicken egg in a ravine. It had a stripe down the middle and it looked like a seed of grain. A passerby bought it from the boys for five kopecks, brought it to the city, and sold it to the Tsar as a rare find.

The Tsar called his wise men and ordered them to find out what it was—an egg or a seed of grain. The wise men thought and thought but could not give an answer. But when the object was placed on the windowsill, a chicken flew inside and began to eat it, and everyone saw that it was grain. So the wise men went to the Tsar and said to him, "This is a grain of rye."

The Tsar was astonished. He asked his wise men to find out where this grain had been grown. The wise men thought and thought, and they searched in their books, but they learned nothing. So they went to the Tsar and said, "We cannot give an answer. There is nothing written in our books about this grain. Therefore, we will have to ask the farmers whether the old men know anything about where and when such grain was grown."

The Tsar sent his servants to bring an old farmer to him. They found such a farmer, a very old man with no teeth and green skin who walked on crutches, and they brought him to the Tsar.

The Tsar showed him the seed of grain, but the old man could not see well, so he half looked at it, half felt it with his hands.

The Tsar asked him, "Tell me, old man, do you know a place where such grain could be grown? Have you grown such a crop in your field? Have you ever purchased such grain from someone else?"

The old man was deaf, and he understood little that was said to him. But he answered, "No, I have neither grown nor gathered such a crop in my field, and I have never purchased such grain. In my time, when bread was made, all the grain was as small as it is now. But you should ask my father. It is possible that he has heard about someone growing such grain."

The Tsar sent for the old man's father. The servants found him, and he came before the Tsar, supporting himself with a crutch. The Tsar showed him the grain. This old man could see better, and he took a good look at it. The Tsar asked him, "Tell me, old man, where was such grain as this grown? Have you grown such a crop in your field? Have you ever purchased such grain from someone else?"

This old man did not hear very well either, but he could hear better than his son. "No," he said, "I have not grown such grain in my field, I have not gathered such a crop, nor have I purchased such grain, because in my time there was no money. Everyone ate the bread they grew themselves and shared with others who were in need. I do not know where such grain could have been grown. Though our grain was bigger than that grown today, I have never seen such big grain. I have heard from my father that, in his time, the grain had a bigger yield and the seeds were bigger than now. You should ask him about it."

The Tsar sent for the old man's father. The third old man came easily to the Tsar, without crutches; he walked with a light step, and his eyes were bright. He could hear very well, and he spoke clearly. The Tsar showed the grain to the old man. He looked at it happily and said, "I have not seen our good old bread for a long, long time." He took a bite of the seed and chewed a little. "Yes, that's it," he said.

So the Tsar asked him, "Tell me please, old man—where was this grain grown? Have you grown such a crop in your field? Did you ever buy such grain from someone else?"

And the old man said to him, "In my time, such grain was everywhere. All my life I ate this grain and fed other people with it."

The Tsar asked, "Please, old man, did you buy this grain somewhere, or did you grow this grain in your field?"

The old man smiled. "In my time," he said, "nobody would even think of committing such a sin as buying or selling grain. We knew nothing of money, and everyone had enough grain for himself. And yes, I have grown and gathered this crop."

And the Tsar said to him, "Old man, tell me, where did you grow this grain, and where was your field?"

And the old man answered, "My field was God's land. Wherever I plowed, there my field was. Land was free. People never claimed land as their own. Only your work belonged to you."

The Tsar said, "Tell me, please, two more things. First, why did such grain grow before in the fields and not now? And the second thing: Why is it that your grandson came on two crutches, and your son came on one crutch, and you come so easily, with clear eyes, strong teeth, and clear speech? How are these two wonders possible?"

And the old man answered, "These two things are possible because people stopped living by their own work and began to steal other people's work. In the past, people lived according to God's will: they claimed only what belonged to them, and they respected property not their own, rather than stealing it."

THE
BERRIES

THE BERRIES

I

It is June, and the days are hot and still. The leaves of the trees are plump and green, and only here and there are seen a few yellowed leaves of linden and birch. The wild rose bushes are covered with fragrant blossoms, and the forest meadows are full of clover. The rye in the fields is getting darker, bigger, and thicker. It moves in waves under the gusts of wind, half ripe, almost ready for harvest. In the ravine the quail are calling, and there are landrails, corncrakes, and grass-drakes in the field. Nightingales sometimes sing out in the forests, then become quiet. The air is dry and very hot. With the slightest puff of wind, the thick layer of dust on the village roads is lifted into the air, either to the right or to the left.

The peasants are busy working, renovating their barns, or taking fertilizer to the fields. The cattle on the dried fields wait for the fresh grass to grow after the first grass was cut. The calves cry *mooo*, with their tails lifted up, and try to run away from the herdsmen. The boys take horses to the ravines, where they graze on the fresh grass. Women haul sacks full of hay from the forest; while young peasant girls play games in the forest clearings. They pick berries and take them to sell to the city people who are staying in their summer cottages or dachas.

The inhabitants of the dachas, the dachniks, live in charming small houses painted in bright colors. They stroll lazily in light, clean, rich clothes under umbrellas to protect themselves from the sun, or tortured by the heat, they sit in the shade of the trees at summer tables, and drink tea or iced drinks.

The luxurious dacha of Nikolai Semyonych has a small tower, a veranda, a small balcony, and galleries. Everything is new, freshly made, and very clean. A troika with groom and bells sits in front of the house; it has brought a gentlemen from St. Petersburg, who paid fifteen rubles "round trip," as the groom says.

The gentleman is a famous liberal activist. He had a hand in the creation of petitions and letters of public support which were so brilliantly written that it seemed that they glorified the government. But in actuality they were letters and petitions of the most liberal nature. He is a very busy man, as always, and before he returns to the city, he will stay for only one day to visit his friend, a childhood schoolmate who shares similar ideas.

They have slightly different views on the constitution. The man from St. Petersburg is more European—and therefore tolerant—in his views on socialism. He is paid a large salary and occupies an important position. Nikolai Semyonych is a purely Russian man, an Orthodox Christian with some Slavophile leanings, and he is a landlord who owns many thousands of acres of land.

They were served a five-course dinner in the garden, but because of the heat they ate almost nothing so that the labors of the expensive cook (who was paid forty rubles) and his several kitchen servants were almost in vain. The diners ate only some beet soup with fresh white fish and some colorful ice cream in a fancy shape decorated with sugar flowers and biscuits. Nikolai Semyonych and his guest were also joined by a liberal doctor, a student with social-democratic views whom Nikolai Semyonych had hired as a tutor for his children, a revolutionary whom Nikolai Semyonych was able to keep in check. Mary, Nikolai's wife, and their three children, the youngest of whom came only for dessert, were also present.

The dinner conversation looked and sounded tense because Mary, a nervous woman by character, was very concerned about

Nicky's diarrhea. Nicky, the youngest boy, was, as always happens in important Russian families, called Nikolai after his father. Mary was also excited because, during the political conversation which had started between the guest and Nikolai Semyonych, the student, wanting to show that he was not ashamed to express his convictions, kept breaking into the discussion and interrupting the guest, until Nikolai Semyonych was able to calm down the revolutionary student.

They dined at seven o'clock. After dinner the friends sat on the veranda, enjoying mineral water with dry white wine, and continued the conversation.

Their difference of opinion mostly manifested itself in the issue of how the elections should be organized—either by direct or electoral vote—and moving into the living room, which was protected from mosquitoes and flies by a net, they began a heated debate. Over tea they discussed a few general questions with Mary, although, distracted by her concern about Nicky's diarrhea, she could not fully participate in the conversation. They spoke about painting, and Mary tried to prove that in decadent painting there is something "Je ne sais quois," and this could not be denied. But she was not really thinking about decadent painting; she had heard what other people had said about decadent art, and simply repeated the same words she had said many times before. The guest spoke in such a way that no one would notice that he had no interest in art at all, either decadent or non-decadent. Nikolai Semyonych, watching his wife, noticed that she was displeased with something, and wondered if something unpleasant were about to happen. Besides that, he was very bored by the things he had heard her say hundreds of times before, or maybe even more.

They lit the expensive bronze lanterns in the backyard because it was getting dark. The children went to bed, and Nicky was given some medicine.

The guest, together with Nikolai Semyonych and the doctor, went onto the veranda. The servant gave them candles and more

mineral water, and when it was already midnight they began a serious lively discussion about the governmental measures which
should be taken in this very important period of Russian history.
Both of them chain-smoked throughout the conversation.

Outside, beyond the gates of the dacha, the horses stood unfed
and jingled their bells, and the groom, also hungry, was either
yawning or snoring. For twenty years he had worked for the same
master, and he sent his whole salary home to his brother, except
for the four or five rubles he spent on vodka. After some time,
when the roosters at nearby dachas started to crow, one of them
with a very loud, high-pitched voice, the groom began to wonder
whether they had completely forgotten about him, so he left the
carriage and went to the dacha. He saw that his passenger was
drinking and saying something in a very loud voice. Becoming
afraid, the groom went to find a house servant. The servant,
dressed in a butler's uniform, was asleep in his chair in the entrance
hall. The groom woke him up. The butler, a former slave, made a
nice living—fifteen rubles in salary from his master plus tips,
sometimes a hundred rubles a year—enabling him to feed his big
family of five daughters and two sons. He jumped up, wide awake,
and went to tell his master that the worried groom was asking to
be relieved.

The servant came into the room in the middle of the discussion. The doctor had joined them earlier, and now the guest was
saying, "I cannot agree that the Russian people should pursue a
different path of development. First of all, there should be freedom, political freedom, which is as important as other basic
human rights." The guest felt confused, as if he had failed to make
his point clearly, but in the heat of the discussion he had forgotten what he was going to say.

"This is true," answered Nikolai Semyonych, whose intention
was to express his own thoughts without listening to other people's
opinions, a mode of conversation he liked very much. "And it is
true that this can be accomplished in some other way—not by a

majority vote, but by a consensus. Look at the decisions made by
the small peasant communities here in Russia."

"Oh, these peasant communities."

"We cannot deny that," said the doctor. "The Slavic people
have their own particular views on life. For example, the Polish
right of political veto—I think this could be much better."

"Let me finish my thought," Nikolai Semyonych said. "The
Russian people have certain qualities. And these qualities—"

At this moment, Ivan the servant came in and said, "The
groom is getting nervous."

The guest from St. Petersburg was very polite to servants and
prided himself on that. "Please tell him," he said, "that I will be
leaving soon. I will pay extra for his time."

"Yes, sir," said Ivan, and went away, and Nikolai Semyonych
finished his thought. But both the guest and the doctor had heard
that thought twenty times—or so it seemed to them—and they
started to argue, especially the guest, citing examples from history.
The guest knew history very well.

The doctor was on the guest's side. He admired the guest's
erudition and wide knowledge and was happy to be acquainted
with such a man.

The conversation lasted so long that dawn began to break
beyond the forest on the other side of the road, and the nightin-
gale woke up and started singing. But the gentlemen kept on
smoking and talking, talking and smoking.

Perhaps this conversation would have continued even longer,
but the maid appeared in the doorway.

This maid was an orphan who had been forced to become a
servant in order to feed herself. First she had worked for a group
of merchants, and the manager forced her to sleep with him, and
she gave birth to a child. Her child died, and she went to work for
a civil servant whose son, a high school student, constantly made
advances, trying to corner her. Coming next to the Nikolai
Semyonych household as junior maid, she found herself very

happy—there were no dissipated masters who persecuted her, and they paid her salary on time. Now she came in to say that the lady was asking for the doctor and for Nikolai Semyonych.

Well, Nikolai Semyonych thought, *maybe something has happened with Nicky.* "What's the problem?" he asked.

"Nikolai Nikolaevich is feeling unwell," said the maid.

"Well, it is time for me to go," the guest said. "Look how light it's getting. We've been sitting for quite a long time, through the night." He smiled to the participants in the conversation, pleased that they had had such a long and peaceful discussion. And then he said goodbye.

Ivan was running about on his old tired feet, looking for the guest's hat and umbrella, which the guest had left in some most unsuitable place. Ivan was hoping for a tip, but the guest, who was usually not greedy and always gave a ruble for a tip, was so involved in the conversation that he completely forgot about this. Only on his way home would he remember that he had not given anything to the servant. "Well, what can I do?" he would say.

The groom climbed onto his carriage, picked up his reins, settled himself comfortably, and urged the horses to go. The bells started ringing. And the guest from St. Petersburg, rocking gently on the soft springs of that exquisite carriage, considered his friend's narrow way of thinking.

Nikolai Semyonych was thinking the same thing about his guest: *What limited views these people from St. Petersburg have! They cannot overcome this.*

He did not go to his wife at once. He was in no hurry because he did not expect anything good from this meeting. The issue was the berries. Yesterday the village children had brought some fresh berries. Nikolai Semyonych had bought two plates of them without bargaining, but the berries were not completely ripe. His children had run up asking for some, and they started eating right from the plates. When, some time later, Mary went out and saw that Nicky had eaten some berries, she became very worried because his stomach was already upset. She reproached her husband, and he reproached her. An unpleasant conversation, almost an argument, followed. In the evening Nicky had a loose stool. Nikolai Semyonych expected that that would be all, but the doctor was called for, and this meant the situation had taken a bad turn.

When Nikolai Semyonych came to his wife, she wore a bright silk gown that he liked very much, but she was not thinking of the gown at the moment. She was standing, together with the doctor, over the child's chamber pot, and she illuminated it inside with a candle.

The doctor was peering very attentively through his glasses, moving the dirty stinking stuff inside the pot with his small stick. "Yes," he said with deep meaning.

"All this is because of those cursed, terrible berries," said the mother.

"Why the berries?" Nikolai Semyonych said timidly.

"Why the berries? You fed him berries, and now I cannot sleep all night. And the child will die," said his wife.

"No, he will not die," said the doctor, smiling. "Just a little bit of bismuth and caution. We will give him the medicine now."

"He just fell asleep," said Mary.

"Then we had better not disturb him. Tomorrow morning I will drop in."

"Please do."

The doctor left. Nikolai Semyonych remained with his wife, and he could not calm her down for a long time. When he finally fell asleep, it was completely light outside.

II

In the neighboring village, beyond the houses, the farmer's children were coming home from their night's work. Some of them were riding and some walking as they brought the horses to the pastures. The foals and colts ran behind them, and a black dog ran in front of the horses, watching them merrily.

Taraska Rezunov, a twelve-year-old boy, barefooted and wearing a peasant coat and a simple cap, was riding a horse that had a small foal. He passed everyone as he galloped uphill to the village. The young horse threw his white legs to this side or that, right or left, when he jumped. Taraska rode to his house, tied the horse's reins to the gates, and went into the front room.

"Hey you, you sleep too much," he shouted at his sisters and brother, sleeping on the carpet. Their mother had slept next to them, but she had already gotten up to milk the cow.

Olga, his sister, jumped up and began to fix her curly long hair with both hands. Fyodor was sleeping, still lying down with his head stuck into his winter coat with which he covered himself at night. His small feet stuck out from under the coat, and he rubbed them one against the other.

The children had made plans the previous night to go and pick berries this morning, and Taraska had promised to waken his sister as soon as he returned from his night's work. He did as he had promised.

Even though he had spent the night sitting in the forest under the bush, nearly falling asleep, now he was full of energy, and he decided not to go to bed, but rather to go with the girls to pick berries. Their mother gave him a glass of milk. He cut himself a chunk of bread, sat down at the table on a bench, and started eating.

By the time he hurried away from the house dressed only in his shirt and pants, the girls were red and white spots on the dark green background of the forest. His bare feet left clear prints behind him in the dust along the road, upon which already lay the distinct prints of even smaller feet. The girls had prepared their cups for berry-picking the evening before, and without eating breakfast or even taking bread for the road, they had crossed themselves twice and run outside. Taraska caught up with them at the edge of the big forest, as soon as they turned from the road.

Everything was covered with dew—the grass, the bushes, and even the lower branches of the trees—and the bare legs of the girls were at first wet and cold, but then became warm from walking on the grass and the uneven, dry soil. The girls first went to an opening in the trees where the forest had recently been cut—it was now a meadow full of berries. The new shoots were just coming up, and between the young bushes, ripening berries, still pinkish-white but sometimes red, were hidden in the low grass.

The young girls bent and picked one berry after another with their small sunburnt hands. The overripe ones they put into their mouths; those that were better, they put into the cups.

"Olga, my dear—come here! There are so many of them!"

"No, here, you liar!"

"Here, come here!" the girls cried to each other from time to time as they went further and further—without going too far into the bushes.

Taraska went further into the ravine, where the forest had been cut about a year before and the young saplings, mostly nut trees and maple trees, had grown taller than he was. The grass was higher and thicker here than anywhere else, and, when he found a strawberry patch, the berries there were larger and much juicier because they were protected by the grass.

"Grusha! Here I am!" Olga called. "What if there is a wolf here?"

"Do you think a wolf would be here? Don't scare me! I am not scared," said Grusha, forgetting about everything else while thinking about the wolf, and putting one berry after another into her mouth instead of into her cup.

"Taraska went across the ravine. Taraska, where are you?"

"Here, come here!" responded Taraska from the other side of the ravine. "Come! Let's go over there, where there are more berries."

Holding onto the bushes, the girls climbed down into the ravine, and then up the other side. There, bathed in bright sunlight, they fell upon a small clearing overflowing with berries. They worked in silence, without stopping, using both hands and lips.

Suddenly something started up, breaking the silence with a thunderous noise in the grass and bushes. Grusha fell, scared almost to death, and half of the berries she had put in her cup fell out on the grass.

"Mama!" she said, beginning to cry.

"It's a hare! Look, it's only a hare! Taraska, look! A hare!" cried Olga, pointing at the gray back with long ears rushing through the bushes.

"Why did you fall?" Olga asked Grusha when the hare disappeared.

"I thought it was the wolf," said Grusha, and as her horror abated, she began laughing through her tears of fright.

"What a silly girl," said Olga.

"I got scared," said Grusha, her thin laughter ringing like a small bell.

They picked up Grusha's berries and went further. The sun rose higher, covering everything in bright patches and shadows. The foliage still glittered with the drops of dew that completely covered the girls as well.

The girls were now on the other side of the forest, but still they went further and further, hoping to find more berries. From various directions they heard the voices of young peasant women and girls who had also gone out to gather berries.

By breakfast time, both the cup and the small pot were half full. And the girls had met another woman, Akulina, who had also come out to pick berries. There was a baby toddling behind Akulina on his curved plump legs, dressed only in his shirt, without any cap. "He decided to follow me," Akulina said, taking the boy into her arms, "and there is no one to leave him with at home."

"And we just scared off a big hare! It made such a great noise in the forest! It was terrible!" Olga said.

"Here you go," Akulina said, lowering the boy to the ground.

After exchanging these words, the girls went in a different direction than Akulina and continued their work.

"Let's sit here for a while," Olga said, sitting down in the shadow of a nut bush. "I feel tired. We should have brought some bread to eat."

"I'm hungry too," said little Grusha.

"Do you hear that? Akulina is yelling something loudly. Do you hear her? Hey, Akulina!"

"Olga, my dear!" answered Akulina.

"What?"

"Is my little one with you?" cried Akulina from behind the bushes.

"No."

Then they heard noises coming from the bushes, and from behind them Akulina appeared, holding the bottom of her skirt up on one side, and holding her basket with her other hand.

"Have you seen my little boy?"

"No."

"What a nuisance. Misha! Misha!"

No one answered.

"Oh, my goodness! He'll get lost and become confused in the big forest."

Olga hurried with Grusha toward one side of the forest, and Akulina went a different way. They kept calling Misha in a loud voice, but no one answered.

"I am so tired," Grusha said, lagging behind. But Olga shouted without stopping; she ran here and there, looking in every direction.

They could hear the desperate voice of Akulina, far away in the forest. Olga wanted to stop looking for the boy and go home, but then she heard the frantic calls of a bird coming from a green bush. Perhaps the bird had some nestlings, and she was angry or afraid of something. Olga studied the small bush, surrounded on all sides by grass white with blossoms, and beneath it she saw a blue lump that did not look like any of the forest herbs. She stooped to have a better look. It was Misha. The bird, afraid of him, was making its call of distress.

Misha lay on his belly, with his arm beneath his head and his plump, curved legs stretched out, and slept soundly.

Olga cried for Misha's mother, woke the little boy, and gave him some berries.

Later, Olga would tell many different people—her neighbors, her mother, her father—again and again the story of how she looked for and found Akulina's tiny son.

The sun came out from behind the trees, baking the ground and everything on it.

"Olga, come have a swim!" the other girls invited her.

They took each other by the hand and went down to the river, singing folk songs. Jumping and yelling, hitting the water with their feet, the girls did not notice a big dark cloud coming from the west. The sun was hidden by the cloud for a moment, then it appeared again, and then again disappeared. The smell of flowers and birch leaves became stronger, and there was the sound of distant thunder. By the time the girls noticed this, it was too late, and the rain soaked them to the skin.

With their skirts and blouses dark with rain and clinging to their bodies, the girls ran home, had a light snack, and then brought dinner to their father, who was plowing the potato field.

By the time they returned home for dinner, their blouses were dry. They sorted the strawberries they had picked, put them into nice cups, and brought them to the dacha of Nikolai Semyonych, where, as a rule, they were usually paid well. This time they had no luck.

Mary was sitting under an umbrella in a large chair, bored by the heat, and when she saw the girls with the berries, she waved her fan at them. "No, no, please don't!"

But Valya, the twelve-year-old eldest son, who had just awakened from the nap he had taken after a tiring day at school and a game of croquet with the neighbor children, saw the berries and ran to Olga and asked her, "How much?"

"Thirty kopecks," she said.

"That's a lot," he said. He said it was a lot because that's what the grown-ups always said. "Well, wait—wait for me behind the corner of the house," he said, and ran to his nanny.

Meanwhile, Olga and Grusha were admiring a glass sphere in which one could see fantastic small houses, forests, and gardens. The glass sphere, and many other things, did not surprise them because they always expected to see something wonderful in this mysterious world, impossible to understand—the world of the rich landowners.

Valya went to his nanny and asked her for thirty kopecks. Saying that twenty kopecks was enough, she took some money from her chest. Valya came back the long way in order to avoid his father, who had just gotten up and, after a difficult night, was smoking and reading newspapers. He gave the twenty-kopeck coin to the girls, then put the berries on a plate and began to eat them.

When they returned home, Olga untied the knot in her handkerchief in which the twenty-kopeck coin was hidden and gave it to her mother. The mother hid the coin and took the laundry to the river.

Taraska, who had been plowing the potato field with his father since early that morning, was now sleeping in the shadow of a large oak tree. His father sat watching the unharnessed horse, which was eating grass at the boundary where his strip of land bordered that of his neighbor. The horse could, at any moment, wander onto someone else's meadow or barley field.

In the family of Nikolai Semyonych, everything was back to normal. Their regular three-course breakfast was ready, but nobody went to the table because nobody wanted to eat.

Having read the day's newspapers, Nikolai Semyonych was satisfied with his political views and judgments, convinced that they were true. Mary was quiet and calm because Nicky had had a good bowel movement. The doctor was satisfied that the measures he had suggested had been effective. Valya was happy because he had eaten the whole plate of strawberries.

STONES

Stones

Two women came to a saintly old man to learn from him. One woman thought herself a great sinner. She had cuckolded her husband when she was young, and she was constantly tortured by her guilt. The other woman had lived all her life according to the law and had committed no serious sins; she did not reproach herself, and she was pleased with her life.

The old man asked both women about their lives. With tears, the first woman immediately confessed her great sin. She told him that she considered her sin so great that she could never be forgiven. The other woman told him that she couldn't think of any particular sins to confess.

To the first woman, the old man said, "Go out behind the fence, servant of God, and find a big stone, as big a stone as you can carry, and bring it to me. And you," he said to the other woman, who did not know of any significant sins to confess, "bring me also as many stones as you can carry, but all of them should be small."

Both women went out and did what he said. The first brought a big stone, the other brought a big sack full of small stones.

The old man looked at the stones and said, "And now, do this: Take these stones and put them back in the same places where you found them. And when you have put them back, come to me again."

The women went to follow the instructions of the old man. The first woman easily found the place from which she had taken the stone, and she put it back where it had been before. The other woman could not remember from which place she had picked up which stone, so without carrying out his order, she returned to the old man with the same sack full of stones.

"The same happens," said the old man, "with your sins. You put the large and heavy stone back in the same place, because you remembered where you had picked it up. Likewise, you remembered your great sin, and you bore the reproaches of other people as well as the reproaches of your conscience. You were humbled by them, and then you could be forgiven of this sin."

"And you," the old man said to the woman who had brought back many small stones, "you could not return the stones to their places because you didn't remember where you had found each small stone. It is the same with your sins. You have sinned in small ways many times. You do not remember those sins, did not confess them, and grew used to a life of sin. In addition, through condemning the sins of others, you have sinned more and more."

We are all sinful, and we will all die and be destroyed if we do not confess our sins.

THE
BIG
DIPPER

The Big Dipper

Long, long ago, there was a great drought on all the earth. The rivers, springs, lakes, and wells dried out, and the grasses, trees, and bushes were burned by the heat of the sun. People and animals died from thirst.

One night a young girl went out from her home with a small dipper to search for water for her sick mother. The girl could find no water anywhere. Becoming tired, she lay down in a grassy field and fell asleep. When she awoke and picked up her dipper, she almost spilled water from it, for it was filled with fresh, clean water. Suddenly joyful, she was about to take a sip, but then decided that she should bring all the water to her mother. She was in such a hurry as she ran home with the dipper that she did not notice a little dog underfoot; she stumbled and dropped the dipper.

The dog squealed pitifully. The girl looked down at her dipper, afraid that she had spilled all of the water, but no, it was standing upright and was still full. She gave some water to the dog, who drank it gratefully. When the girl again picked up the dipper, she saw that it had turned from wood into silver.

The girl brought the dipper home and took it to her mother. But her mother said, "I have to die anyway, so you should drink the water yourself," and gave the dipper back to her daughter. Instantly, the silver dipper turned to gold.

The girl could not hold back any longer, and just as she was about to drink, a pilgrim came to their home and asked for water.

Before she took a sip herself, she gave the dipper to him. Suddenly, seven huge diamonds appeared on the dipper, and a stream of clear, fresh water poured from it.

Those seven diamonds rose higher and higher until they sparkled in the sky, becoming the constellation we call the Big Dipper.

THE
POWER OF
CHILDHOOD

The Power of Childhood

S hoot him! Kill him now! Shoot him on the spot! Cut his throat! He's a murderer! Let's kill him! Kill him!"

These were the shouts from the huge crowd of people that were leading a man down the street, his hands bound with rope. The man was tall and straight, and he stepped forward firmly, holding his head high. It was clear, on his strong, handsome face, that he despised and hated the people who surrounded him.

This man was one of those who, during the people's rebellion against the government, had fought on the side of the government. Now they had caught him, and were bringing him to execution.

What can I do now? thought the man. *Well, one cannot win all the time. I can do nothing—these people are in power for the moment. Perhaps it is my time to die. This may be my destiny.* He shrugged his shoulders and responded with a cold and indifferent smile to the shouts and yells from the crowd.

"This is a police officer! Just this morning he was shooting at us!" he heard someone cry.

The crowd pressed forward relentlessly, carrying him further along. When they came to the street where the dead bodies of the people killed yesterday by the government's forces were still piled on the sidewalk, the crowd became furious. "Why wait? Don't delay this! Shoot him now! Why take him elsewhere?" yelled people from the crowd.

The prisoner frowned and lifted his head even higher, as if he hated this crowd even more than they hated him.

"Kill them all! Kill the spies! The kings! The ministers! And these scoundrels! Kill them all!" shrieked several hysterical women. But the crowd's leaders decided to bring him to the city square and finish with him there.

They were not far from the city square when, in a quieter moment, they heard a sobbing child's voice crying from the back of the crowd. "Daddy! Daddy!" cried a six-year-old boy, sobbing and pushing himself through the crowd to get closer to the prisoner. "Daddy! What are they going to do to you? Wait, wait, take me with you, take me!"

The yells and shouts of the angry people stopped near where the child was, and the crowd separated before the child to let him pass through, as if he had some power over them. They allowed the child to approach closer and closer to his father.

"Such a nice boy! Just look at him! What a dear little boy!" a woman said.

"Who are you calling?" another woman said, leaning over the boy.

"Daddy! I want to go with Daddy!" he squealed.

"How old are you, boy?"

"What are you doing to my daddy?" the boy replied.

"Go home, boy—go to your mother," one of the men from the crowd said.

But the prisoner had heard his son's voice, and he had heard what the people had told him. His face became even gloomier. "He has no mother!" he shouted, in answer to the man who had just spoken.

The boy pushed himself further through the crowd. At last he reached his father and climbed into his arms. The crowd resumed its imprecations: "Kill him! Hang him! Shoot the scoundrel!"

"Why did you leave the house?" the father asked.

"What are they going to do to you?" the boy said.

"Listen, I want you to do something for me."

"What?"

"Do you know Catherine?"

"Our neighbor? Sure I do."

"Then listen. Go and stay with her. And I—I will come back soon."

"I won't go without you," the boy said, starting to cry.

"Why? Why won't you go?"

"They will kill you."

"No, this is nothing. They are just playing." The prisoner put the boy down and approached the man who led the crowd.

"Listen," he said, "You can kill me however you want and wherever you want, but don't do this in the child's presence," and he gestured toward the boy. "Untie me for two minutes and hold my hand. I will tell him that you are my friend and that we are going for a stroll, and then he will leave us. And then . . . and then you can kill me, in any way you want."

The leader of the crowd agreed.

Then the prisoner again took the boy by his hands and said, "Be a good boy—go to Catherine."

"But what about you?"

"See, this friend and I are taking a walk. We will go a little further while you go home, and I'll come in a little while. Go on, be a good boy."

The boy stared at his father, then he tilted his head to one side, and then to the other. He thought for a moment. "Will you come back?"

"Go on, my dear. I will come soon."

"Will you?" And the child obeyed his father.

A woman led him out of the crowd.

When the child had disappeared from his sight the prisoner said, "Now I am ready. You can kill me."

And then something happened, something inexplicable and unexpected. In one instant, the same spirit awoke in all these cruel, merciless people filled with hatred. One woman said, "You know what? Let's let him go."

"God will be his judge. Let him go," agreed someone else.

"Let him go! Let him go!" the crowd shouted.

And this proud man, who had hated this crowd a moment ago, began to sob. He put his hands over his face, and like someone guilty, he ran through the crowd, and no one stopped him.

WHY DID IT HAPPEN?

Why Did It Happen?

I

In the spring of 1830, Mr. Jachevsky had a visitor to his estate: Joseph Migursky, the only son of an old friend who had died long ago. Mr. Jachevsky was sixty-five years old. A patriot from the period of the second division of Poland, he had a big forehead, wide shoulders, a large chest, and a long white mustache on his dark brown face. He had served under the banners of Ko´sciuszko, along with Mr. Migursky the senior when they were both young men, and with all the force of his patriotic soul he hated the apocalyptic and dissipated Russian Tsarina Catherine II, as he called her, with her traitor-lover Poniatkovsky. He believed in the rebirth of the great Polish state, *Rzezc Pospolita,* as firmly as he believed that the sun would rise in the sky the next morning. In 1812, he had commanded a regiment in Napoleon's army, and he had adored the French emperor. After Napoleon's death he was very sad, but he had not completely despaired of the rebirth and recreation of the terribly injured but still extant kingdom of Poland. His hope had been rekindled when Alexander the First opened the Seim, the Polish Parliament, in Warsaw, but the holy union of the reactionary forces in Europe and the stupid politics pursued by Konstantin had made the realization of his sacred wish more distant.

Since 1825, Jachevsky had lived in the countryside, on his estate Rozhanka, and kept busy with hunting, managing the estate, and reading all the newspapers and letters through which he attentively followed the events in his motherland. He was married for the second time to a rather beautiful aristocratic lady from a poor family, but this marriage was not happy. He did not love her; he did not even respect her. He treated her badly and abused her, as if he wanted to pay her back for the mistake he had made in his second marriage. They had no children. His first wife had given him two daughters. The older was named Vanda, a girl of stately beauty who was bored by the country life; the younger daughter, Albina, his beloved child, was a lively, thin girl with long, curly, blond hair and huge shining blue eyes, rather widely spaced in the same way as her father's.

Albina was fifteen years old when Joseph Migursky came to visit. Before this, as a student, Mr. Migursky had come to visit the Jachevsky family in Vilno, where they stayed in the winter, and he had tried to flirt with Vanda then. But now he came as a grown-up and independent young man visiting them for the first time at their countryside estate.

Young Migursky's visit was enjoyable for all the residents of Rozhanka. The old man was pleased that the young Migursky looked exactly like his father, his childhood friend, and that with passion and rosy hopes he spoke about the revolutionary excitement not only in Poland, but even in the places abroad where Migursky had just been. Mrs. Jachevsky liked Migursky as well, because when guests came to visit them, old Mr. Jachevsky became more reserved and did not scold her as usual. Vanda was pleased because she was sure that Migursky had come for her and was intending to propose to her. She was going to accept his proposal, but she was planning, as she said to herself, *lui tenir la dragée haute*, to sell her freedom for a high price. Albina was happy because everybody else was happy. Not only Vanda believed that Migursky had come to propose to her. Everybody in the house thought the same, from the old Mr. Jachevsky to their maid Ludviga, though nobody said this out loud.

And it was true. Migursky had originally come with this intention, but after spending a week at the estate, he became disappointed and upset with something, and then went away without making a proposal. Everyone was surprised by this strange departure, and nobody except Albina knew that she, Albina, had caused it. All the time he was at Rozhanka, she had noticed that Migursky was especially excited and cheerful only with her. He treated her as a child, he joked with her and made fun of her, but she felt with a woman's intuition that the way he related to her was not the attitude of a grown man toward a child, but rather that of a man toward a woman. She recognized this in the admiring glance and tender smile with which he greeted her every time she entered the room and with which he saw her off when she departed. She did not know what his exact attitude toward her was, but his excitement made her feel happy, and so she involuntarily did the things he liked. And he liked all the things she did; therefore, in his presence she did everything she had done before but with even more excitement. He liked to watch when she raced with her wonderful borzoi, who jumped at her shoulders and licked her shining, smiling face; he liked to hear her voice when she burst out laughing under any pretext with a wonderfully beautiful ringing laughter; he liked to look at her when the priest was giving a dull sermon in the church and, while her eyes were laughing, she pretended to be serious; he liked it when she comically imitated the behavior of an old nanny, or of a drunk neighbor, or of him—Mr. Migursky instantly moving from one impression to another. Most of all, he liked her love of life, as if she had just discovered the beauty of life and was trying to enjoy it. This love of life grew greater and greater just because she knew that it delighted him.

Therefore, only Albina knew why Migursky, though he had come to make a proposal to Vanda, had departed without doing it. She was not brave enough to admit it to anyone—she did not say it even to herself—but deep in her soul she knew that he had wanted to fall in love with her sister, but instead he had fallen in love with her, Albina. She was greatly surprised by this, thinking that she was nothing in comparison with the clever, well-educated, and beautiful Vanda. But she could not help believing it, and she felt so happy because, with all her heart, she was in love with Migursky. She loved him deeply, as a person can be deeply in love only for the first time, and only once in her life.

II

By the end of the summer, the papers brought news about the revolution in Paris. Afterwards came news of preparations for a rebellion in Warsaw. Mr. Jachevsky awaited, with both fear and hope, news of the assassination of Konstantin Pavlovich, which would begin a Polish revolution. In November, they heard about the attack on the royal palace, and the escape of Konstantin, and that the Polish Seim had voted for the dethronement of the Romanovs. Hlopitsky was pronounced a dictator, and the Polish people were free again.

The rebellion did not reach Rozhanka, but all the inhabitants of the estate observed it, expected it, and prepared for it. Old Mr. Jachevsky wrote letters to a friend, one of the leaders of the rebellion, made appointments, and received some mysterious Jewish bankers, not in connection with his estate management, but about financing the revolutionary uprising. He was ready to join the rebellion as soon as the time came. Mrs. Jachevsky paid more attention than usual to the material comfort of her husband, and by doing so she irritated him even more. Vanda sent all her jewelry and diamonds to their friend in Warsaw, so that the money received from its sale could be given to the revolutionary committee. Albina was interested in only one thing: what activity Migursky was engaged in. She found out through her father that he had entered Dvernitsky's battalion, so she tried to find out everything she could about this military detachment.

Migursky wrote only twice. In the first letter, he wrote that he had joined the army; in his second letter, in the middle of February, he wrote a long and exciting account of the Polish victory at Stocheck, where they captured six Russian cannons and some prisoners of war. He wrote, "Victory for Poland and defeat for Moscow! Hooray!" With those words he finished the letter.

Albina was excited. She examined the map, calculating when and where the Muscovites should be completely defeated; she grew pale and trembled every time her father opened packages that came in the mail. Once her stepmother entered her room and caught her standing in front of the mirror in pants and a uniform hat. Albina was planning to dress in men's clothing and run away from home to join the Polish army. Her stepmother told her father. Mr. Jachevsky invited his daughter to his room. Trying to mask his sympathy and even his admiration, he reprimanded her sternly, insisting that she drive thoughts about participating in the war out of her head. "A woman has more important things to do. She should love and take care of those who sacrifice themselves for their motherland," he told her. For now, she was necessary to him, as his joy and solace. And the time would come when her husband would need her. Her father knew how to influence Albina. He hinted that he was alone and unhappy, and he kissed her. She pressed her face against him, hiding the tears that wet the sleeve of his gown anyway, and she promised him to do nothing without his consent.

III

Only Poles who had experienced the division of Poland, and the submission of one part of it to the Germans, whom the Poles hated, and the other part to the Muscovites, whom they hated even more—only these Poles could understand the joy that the Polish people felt in 1830 and 31, when after previous unsuccessful attempts at liberation, the hope of freedom seemed realizable. But this hope did not last for long. The Russian forces were superior, and the revolution was again suppressed. And again, completely obedient to their orders, tens of thousands of Russian people moved into Poland under the leadership of generals Dibich and Paskevich and under the supreme command of Nikolai I, and without knowing why, they soaked the earth with their own blood and the blood of their brothers the Poles. And the Russians smashed the Poles and delivered them back into the power of weak and insignificant people who desired neither freedom nor the suppression of the Poles but only one thing: to satisfy their greed and their childish vanity.

Warsaw, the capital, was taken. All the small detachments were defeated. Hundreds, even thousands, of people were executed by firing squads, or beaten to death, or sent to prison and exile. Among those exiled was the young Mr. Migursky. His estate was confiscated, and he was sent as a soldier to an infantry battalion in Uralsk City, in western Siberia.

The Jachevskys lived in Vilno throughout the winter of 1832 to improve the health of the old man, who had been suffering from heart disease since 1831. There they received a letter from Migursky, sent from the fortress in Siberia. He wrote that it was difficult for him to endure everything he had experienced and would experience, but he was happy with the thought that he suffered for his motherland, and he did not despair about the holy cause for which he had sacrificed part of his life. He was ready to sacrifice the rest of his life, and if the opportunity arose tomorrow, he would do the same. Reading the letter aloud, the old man began to weep when he came to this part and could not continue. In the second part of the letter, which Vanda read aloud, Migursky wrote that *whatever plans and dreams* he'd had during his last visit—which would always stand out as the brightest spot in his life—he could not and did not want to speak about them now.

Both Vanda and Albina understood these words in their own way, but they did not reveal to anyone just how they understood them. At the end of the letter, Migursky sent his regards to everyone—then, in the same joking tone with which he had treated

Albina during that last visit, he addressed her in this letter, asking whether she still ran as fast as she did before, faster than the borzoi, and whether she could still imitate other people. He wished the old man health, he wished his wife success in the running of the household affairs, he wished Vanda a worthy husband, and he wished Albina a continuing joie de vivre.

IV

The health of the old Mr. Jachevsky grew worse and worse, and in 1833 the whole family went abroad. Vanda met a rich Polish immigrant in Baden-Baden and married him. The old man's health deteriorated even further, and early that year he died abroad in Albina's arms. He did not let his wife take care of him, nor did he ever forgive her for the mistake he made in marrying her. Old Mrs. Jachevsky returned with Albina to their estate. The major interest of Albina's life was Migursky. In her eyes, he was the greatest hero and martyr, to whom she decided to dedicate her whole life. Even before she went abroad, she began corresponding with him, first on behalf of her father, and then on her own. After her father's death she returned to Russia and continued writing him. When she was eighteen years old, she announced to her stepmother that she had decided to go to Uralsk to marry Migursky. The stepmother claimed that Migursky selfishly wanted only to improve his difficult situation by marrying a rich young lady and forcing her to share his misfortunes. Becoming angry, Albina declared to her stepmother that only she could have such terrible thoughts about a man who had sacrificed everything for his people, that Migursky, to the contrary, had refused all the assistance she had offered him, and that she had finally decided to go see him and to marry him, if he would agree to give her this happiness. Albina was of age, and she had some money: three hundred thousand gold coins that her uncle had left to his two nieces as their inheritance. So nothing could stop her.

In November of 1833, Albina said goodbye to her family, who saw her off as if she were going to die in that remote part of the world, the barbarian Muscovite state. She sat in her father's newly repaired carriage with Ludviga, the old maid she took with her, and set off on her long journey.

V

Migursky did not live in the soldier's barracks but instead rented his own apartment. Tsar Nikolai Pavlovich had ordered that the demoted Polish officers should be sent to exile as soldiers, where they would be humiliated, enduring the same difficulties as the privates. But most of the people who carried out these orders understood the difficult position of these former officers, and in spite of the danger of being punished for not obeying the Tsar's command, tried to follow their common sense. The commander of the battalion in which Migursky served was a former soldier himself; he could hardly read, but he perfectly understood the situation of this formerly rich and well-educated young man who had now lost everything. He pitied and respected Migursky, and gave him an easier life than the other soldiers. Migursky could not help appreciating the kindness of this colonel, with his white whiskers on a big, plump soldier's face, so he agreed to teach mathematics and French to both of the colonel's sons, who were preparing to enter the officer's school.

Migursky had been living for seven months in Uralsk, and it was a very monotonous, uninteresting life, filled with hardships. Besides the commander of his battalion, with whom he tried to keep a very distant relationship, his only friend was an exiled Polish officer who did not have a good education, a rather unpleasant person who started a fish trade in this small town. The greatest difficulty in Migursky's life was that he could not get used to being in need. After his estate was confiscated, he had no money, and he supported himself for some time by selling the few golden trinkets he had left.

The only great joy in his life was correspondence with Albina, whose poetic and lovely image had remained in his soul since his visit to the Rozhanka estate, and which here in exile became more and more beautiful in his memories. In one of her first letters, she asked him what his words in one of his previous letters meant: "no matter what my wishes and dreams might have been." He responded by confessing to her that he had dreamed about her becoming his wife. She answered that she loved him. He replied that it would be better if she did not write this because it was torturous to think about what might have been and was now impossible. She responded that, not only was it possible, but that it would certainly happen. He wrote that he could not accept her sacrifice, and that his present situation made it completely impossible.

Soon after this letter, he received a check by mail for two thousand zloty. From the stamp and the handwriting on the envelope, he knew that the letter was from Albina, and he remembered that in one of his first letters he had written jokingly that he took special joy in giving lessons, thus making some money for his tea, tobacco, and even books. So he put the check into another envelope with a letter in which he asked her not to spoil their beautiful and holy relationship with money. He wrote that he had enough of everything and was happy just to have such a good friend as she. At this point their correspondence stopped.

In November, Migursky sat at the colonel's house giving a lesson to his sons when he heard the ringing bells of an approaching postal carriage. Squeaking on the frosty snow, the sledge stopped in front of the entrance. The children jumped up to find out who was visiting them. Migursky stayed in the room, waiting for the children to return, but the colonel's wife entered the room instead.

"My dear sir," she said, "there are two ladies asking for you, and it seems that they are from your country—they appear to be Polish."

If someone had asked Migursky whether it was possible for Albina to visit him, he would have answered that it was impossible, but deep in his soul he wanted it to be true. The blood rushed to his heart; out of breath, he ran out into the entrance hall. There he saw a rather fat old woman with a dark pockmarked face, taking off her shawl. The other woman was just entering the colonel's house. When she heard his steps behind her, she looked back, and Migursky saw, full of joy for life, the widely set, shining blue eyes of Albina, her eyelashes covered with frost. He was frozen with amazement, and he did not know what to do and how to greet her.

"Joe!" she shouted, using the name her father had called him by, the one she had used all the time, and she threw her arms around his neck and pressed her flushed, cold face to his, laughing and crying at the same time.

The colonel's wife, when she found out who Albina was and the purpose of her visit, invited her to stay in her house until their marriage.

VI

The kindhearted colonel wrote letters to the upper command, and they received permission for Migursky and Albina to marry. They sent for a Polish priest from the city of Orenburg, and he performed the marriage ceremony for the Migurskys. The commander's wife acted as Albina's mother, one of his students carried the icon, and Brzozovsky, another exiled Polish officer, was the witness.

Albina, though it may seem strange, passionately loved her husband, even though before the ceremony she hardly knew him. Only now did she discover who he really was. It goes without saying that in this real man of flesh and blood, she discovered many rank-and-file, nonpoetic things that had not existed in the poetic image she had nurtured in her imagination for so long. But exactly because this was a real man of flesh and blood, she discovered many simple and good things in him that she had not suspected before, in her abstract understanding of him. She had previously heard from friends and acquaintances that he had been a truly brave man during the war, and she also knew that he had been brave when he lost his freedom and his estate, and so she had imagined him as a hero living an elevated, heroic life. In reality, it turned out that in spite of all his great physical strength and bravery, he was at the same time a humble and quiet man, as quiet as a lamb, a simple person with very simple jokes, a man whose sensitive lips formed a childish smile between the blond beard and mustache which had attracted her back in Rozhanka—a man with a pipe he smoked all the time, a pipe she could not bear when she was pregnant.

Migursky, too, got to know Albina only now, and in her he discovered a woman for the first time—something he did not know even though he had known other women before their marriage. In Albina he discovered things that, though common to women, nevertheless surprised him and might have disillusioned him with women in general if he hadn't felt a certain tender and grateful feeling toward Albina. Toward Albina, as toward women in general, he felt an affectionate, somewhat ironic indulgence. But toward Albina as an individual he felt not only tender love, but also delight and a sense of indebtedness for her sacrifice, which had given him such undeserved happiness.

The Migurskys found great happiness in directing all the energy of their love toward each other. Around other people they felt like two souls lost somewhere in winter, giving warmth to each other. The Migurskys' joyful life was enriched by the presence of their nurse, Ludviga, a good-natured, querulous, and comic figure who fell in love with every man she met and was totally devoted to her mistress. The Migurskys were happy, too, with their children. A year after their wedding a boy was born, and a year and a half later, a girl. The boy was the spitting image of his mother— the same eyes and the same liveliness and graciousness. The girl was a healthy and beautiful little creature.

The Migurskys were unhappy to be so far from their motherland, and they also struggled with the hardships of their unusual and oppressive situation. Albina especially suffered from this oppression because this was her Joe, her hero, who now had to stand at attention before any officer, do rifle drills, serve as a guard, and submissively obey any command.

In addition, they received the saddest news from Poland: Almost all their family and friends had either been exiled or had lost everything and emigrated abroad. For the Migursky family, there was no hope for any improvement of their situation. All of Migursky's attempts to petition for pardon or at least a promotion to an officer's rank led to nothing. Nikolai Pavlovich did military inspections, exercises, and parades, flirted with women at masked balls, and made long trips across Russia, from Chuguev to Novorossisk, from St. Petersburg to Moscow, instilling fear in the people and killing more and more horses by riding them to death. But whenever some brave man asked him to show compassion to the exiled Decembrists, or to the Polish officers who had suffered for their love of their motherland, a quality he admired and praised so highly, then he took a deep breath, looked at that man with his frozen eyes, and said, "Let them continue their service. It is still early." As if he knew when it would not be too early, and when it would be the right time. And all the generals and the senior officers and their wives, and the other people who received their salary from him, admired the sagacity and wisdom and intellect of this great man.

All in all, the Migursky family had more happiness than unhappiness.

They lived like this for five years. But then they suffered an unexpected and terrible misfortune. First, the girl fell ill, followed two days later by the boy. He burned with fever for three days, and without medical assistance (for they could not find a doctor), on the fourth day he died. The girl died two days later.

Albina did not drown herself in the Ural River, but only because she could imagine her husband's horror when he found out about her suicide. Still, it was difficult for her to live. Before, she had been very active in taking care of the household, but now, she shifted all her work to Ludviga. She would sit for hours doing nothing, looking silently at whatever happened to be in front of her, and then suddenly she would jump up and run to her room, staying there without answering Ludviga's or her husband's questions, crying silently, asking them to leave her alone. In the summer she went to her children's graves and sat torturing herself with thoughts of what might have been. Most of all, she was tortured by the thought that her children might have lived if their family had lived in a city where there might have been medical treatment.

Why? Why did it happen? she asked herself. *Neither Joe nor I want anything from anyone, except for him to live as his grandparents and great-grandparents lived, and me to live with my husband and love him and my children and bring them up. Instead, they tortured him, sent him into exile, and then they took from me the most precious thing in the world, the lives of my children. Why? What for?* She asked this question of both people and God, but she received no answer.

And without this answer, there was no life. Life had stopped for Albina. This poor and limited life in exile, which she had tried to decorate with grace and good taste, this life became unbearable not only for her, but for Migursky as well, who suffered with her and did not know how to help her.

VII

At this very difficult time for the Migursky family, another Pole, Mr. Rosolovsky, came to Uralsk City. He had been involved in a grand conspiracy of Polish officers to start a rebellion and escape from Siberia. The head of the conspiracy was a Polish priest, Sirotsinsky, who was also an exile in Siberia.

Rosolovsky, like Migursky and many other people, had been exiled to Siberia for his desire to maintain his Polish national identity. He was punished for his involvement in the conspiracy by being beaten and sent as a soldier to the same battalion in which Migursky served. A former math teacher, Rosolovsky was a tall, slightly hunchbacked, thin man with sunken cheeks and a frowning forehead.

During the first night of his visit, sitting in the Migurskys' room having tea, Rosolovsky spoke in a slow, quiet, low voice about the plan for which he had suffered so much. He told them that the priest Sirotsinsky had organized a secret society throughout Siberia, the purpose of which was, with the help of the Poles who had been enlisted in the Russian army, both in the Cossack detachments and the infantry regiments, to incite the soldiers and prisoners and then the local population to revolt, and then to capture the artillery in Omsk and free everyone.

"Was that ever really possible?" asked Migursky.

"The plan was very realistic, everything was ready," said Rosolovsky with a grim frown. Slowly, calmly, he told them the details of the plan to liberate the Poles in Siberia, and of the measures that had been taken to ensure the success of this enterprise, and of the backup plan to save the organizers of the rebellion in case it was unsuccessful.

"It would have been a sure success if only two scoundrels had not betrayed us," Rosolovsky insisted. He also claimed that Sirotsinsky had been a true hero, a spiritual giant who had died as a martyr. And Rosolovsky related in his low, quiet voice the details of the execution, which he had been forced to witness, of Sirotsinksy and other people who were being prosecuted in this criminal case.

"Two battalions of soldiers stood in two rows along a very long street, and every soldier had in his hand a very strong stick, flexible and thick. The thickness of the sticks was prescribed by the Tsar, so that three sticks could just barely fit into the rifle's muzzle.

"Dr. Shakalsky was the first to go. Two soldiers supported him, one on either side. The soldiers who had the sticks beat him on his bare back as he passed through. I saw him only when he came near the place I stood. Before that, I heard only the noise of the drumbeat, but when I heard the whistle of the sticks hitting his body, I knew he was approaching. I saw that two soldiers had fixed his arms and shoulders to a long rifle, and they dragged him along, quivering and turning his head to this or the other side at each blow.

"As they pulled him past us, I heard a Russian doctor say to the soldiers, 'Do not hit him so painfully—please take pity on him!' But they beat him with great force. When they led him by me for the second time, he could not even walk, and they were dragging him. It was terrible to look at his back. I closed my eyes. Then he fell on the ground, and they carried him away.

"Then they brought the second person, then the third, then the fourth. Everybody fell, and everybody was carried away, some dead and others barely alive. And we all had to stand and watch. The execution went on for six hours, from early in the morning till two in the afternoon.

"The priest Sirotsinsky was the last person to go through this punishment. I had not seen him for a long time, and I did not recognize him at first that day, because during this period of time he had grown very old. His wrinkled face was very pale and greenish in hue. His naked body was thin and yellow, and his ribs stuck out above his sagging stomach. With every blow, he trembled and moved his head abruptly, as the others had, but he did not moan, and he recited the prayer 'Miserere mei Deus'—'Forgive me, oh Lord, according to your great mercy.'

"I heard it myself," Rosolovsky said, murmuring slowly, and then he closed his mouth and started to breathe loudly through his nose.

Ludviga, sitting next to the window, started to cry, covering her face with a handkerchief.

"Oh, stop talking about these terrible details! They are animals, they are real animals—that's what they are!" said Migursky, and putting away his pipe, he jumped up from his chair and strode quickly into the dark bedroom. Albina sat without moving, staring into the dark corner.

VIII

The next day, Migursky came home after his military exercises and was surprised when his wife greeted him with a cheerful face, the way she used to, and led him to the bedroom.

"Joe, listen to me."

"I'm listening. What?"

"All through this night I thought about what Rosolovsky told us yesterday, and I decided that I cannot live like this any longer. I simply cannot. I would rather die than stay here."

"What can we do?"

"We have to escape."

"Escape? How?"

"I have figured it all out. Listen." And she told him the plan she had come up with during the night: He, Migursky would leave their house late at night and leave his soldier's coat on the bank of the Ural River, with a letter in the coat saying that he had committed suicide. They would think that he had drowned in the river. They would search for a body, they would send letters everywhere, but she would hide him so that nobody would be able to find him. He could live comfortably for a month or so in hiding. When everything had calmed down, they would escape.

When he first heard it, this idea seemed impossible to Migursky, but she continued to plead her case with great passion and determination, and by the end of the day, he agreed. His reason for agreeing was that, although the punishment for attempting to escape was the same as that Rosolovsky had described, if their escape attempt should fail only he alone, Migursky, would be punished. His death would make her free, and he knew that life had been very difficult for her since the death of the children.

They told Rosolovsky and Ludviga about their idea, and after many conversations and discussions and changes of small details, the final plan was worked out.

The first step was to fake Migursky's suicide. Once he had been officially declared drowned, he would secretly go to a predetermined place, where Albina would pick him up in a carriage. That was their first plan. But then Rosolovsky told them about the numerous attempts to escape from Siberia during the past five years. Almost all had failed—only one lucky person had managed to escape with his life.

So Albina suggested another plan: Joe, hidden in the carriage, would go with her and Ludviga up to Saratov, a city on the Volga River. In Saratov she would hire a boat and go down the Volga River to some particular place they would select. After dressing in disguise, he would walk along the bank of the river and meet her there, and then they would sail together down the river to the Astrakhan, and then to the Caspian Sea and Persia. Everyone supported this plan, especially Mr. Rosolovsky, who had generated most of the ideas. But it would be difficult to create a hiding place inside the carriage that would not attract the attention of the police but would still be big enough to hide a person. When, after visiting the grave of her children, Albina told Rosolovsky that it would be painful for her to leave the bodies of her children in a faraway country, he said, "Ask the chief's permission to take the coffins of your children with you, and he will allow you."

"No. I do not want to, I do not want to," Albina said.

"Ask for permission, I tell you. This is the solution. You won't actually take the coffins, but we will make a big wooden box for them, and hide Joe in the box."

At first Albina refused this suggestion because it was painful for her to connect this deceit with the memory of her children. But when Migursky joyfully and optimistically supported the idea, she finally agreed.

Their final plan was as follows: Migursky would trick his commanding officers into believing that he had drowned himself. After his death had been accepted and officially confirmed, Albina would write a letter saying that because of the death of her husband, she wished permission to return home to her motherland, and to take the remains of her children with her. When she had received this permission, they would pretend that both graves had been exhumed and the coffins removed, but the coffins would be left in their places, and Migursky would be concealed in the wooden box prepared for the children's coffins. The box would be put into the carriage, and they would go to Saratov. In Saratov they would hire a boat. In the boat, Joe would be free to get out of the box, and they would float down the river to the Caspian Sea, and then go either to Persia or Turkey—and freedom.

IX

First the Migurskys bought a carriage, under the pretext of sending Ludviga home to Poland. Then they started building a special box for the carriage in which a person could lie down and hide—although in a crooked position—and not suffocate. He would also need to be able to easily and inconspicuously get in and out. All three of them—Albina, Rosolovsky, and Migursky himself—came up with the design and put the box together. The assistance of Rosolovsky was very important because he turned out to be a good carpenter. The box was constructed in such a way that it could be easily attached to the rear of the carriage, very tightly and neatly. The wall of the box adjacent to the back of the carriage was removable, so that the person in the box could lie down, partially in the box and partially on the bottom of the carriage, under the seats. In addition, several holes were bored in the box for ventilation. On the outside, the box would be covered with thick cotton cloth and tied with ropes. One could get in and out only through the carriage, from under the seat.

When the carriage and the box were ready, but before her husband disappeared, Albina visited the colonel to prepare him. She told him that her husband had become depressed and melancholic, that he had lost interest in life, and that he had tried to commit suicide. She said that she was afraid for him and asked the colonel to allow him some vacation time. She had a gift for drama, and her excitement and fear for her husband were so natural that the colonel was touched, and he promised to do everything he could. Then Migursky wrote the letter that was to be found in the cuff of his soldier's coat on the banks of the Ural River.

On the predetermined date, he went to the Ural River, waited until darkness, took off his dress and his coat, left them on the bank of the river with the letter inside the coat, and secretly returned home. They hid him in a place under the roof, the door to which was secured with a lock. During the night, Albina sent Ludviga to the colonel to tell him that her husband had left home about twenty hours before and had not returned. In the morning, they brought her the letter from her husband, and with an expression of great despair, she tearfully showed it to the colonel. A week later, Albina sent an official letter asking for permission to go home to her motherland. Mrs. Migursky's grief made an impression on everyone who saw her. They all felt sorry for the unhappy mother and wife. When permission was granted for her departure, she wrote another letter, asking permission to exhume the bodies of her children and take them with her. The local authorities were astonished by this sentimental wish, but they gave their permission.

Two days later, Rosolovsky, together with Albina and Ludviga, went to the cemetery in a hired cart that contained the box for the coffins of the children. Albina knelt before her children's graves and prayed. Then she stood up quickly, and frowning, addressed Rosolovsky. "Do what needs to be done, but I cannot stay here," and she walked off to the side.

Rosolovsky and Ludviga moved the tombstones and dug out the topsoil, so that it looked as if the graves had been opened. When they were finished, they called to Albina, and then returned home with the box filled with soil.

The day chosen for their departure arrived. Rosolovsky was happy, anticipating the success of their venture. Ludviga baked many cookies and pastries for the road, all the while repeating her favorite proverb, "Iak mame kocham." She said that her heart was breaking with fear and joy. Migursky, too, was filled with joy over the possibility of freedom, happy to leave the attic where he had stayed for more than a month, but, most of all, he was buoyed by Albina's optimism and joie de vivre. It seemed that Albina had forgotten about her former sorrow and about all the dangers. Now, she ran to his hiding place shining with the enthusiastic joy of her girlhood days.

At three o'clock in the morning, a Cossack arrived with a troika of horses. Albina and Ludviga sat on the carriage, together with a small dog, on cushions covered with a carpet. The Cossack and the groom sat in the coach box. Migursky, in peasant dress, lay in the back, in the trunk of the carriage.

They left the city, and the troika pulled the carriage along a firm road as hard as stone, along the endless, unplowed steppe, covered with silver leaves of feather grass.

X

It seemed to Albina that the heart in her breast stood still from hope and excitement. She wanted to share her feelings, and she sometimes smiled at Ludviga, nodding either at the wide back of the Cossack in front of her, who was sitting on the groom's seat, or at the bottom of the carriage. Ludviga sat motionless with an expression of great importance, looking straight in front of her and just slightly pursing her lips.

It was a very clear day. The limitless, empty steppe, its silver feather grass shining in the slanting, horizontal rays of the morning sun, unfolded on all sides. The quick, unforged feet of the Bashkir horses resonated on the hard road, along which Albina could see the small hills of soil created by gophers. Very far away on the steppe, she could see the small animals standing on their back feet, whistling piercingly, warning others about the danger, then hiding in their holes. Occasionally they met other Cossacks with caravans of wheat, or Bashkir riders whom the Cossack greeted in the Tartar language.

At all the horse stations where they stopped, the horses were fresh and well fed. Albina gave fifty kopecks for vodka to the grooms, and so they drove, as they called it, at the speed of special delivery mail—that is, they galloped all the way at top speed.

At the first horse station, when the old groom took away the tired horses and the new groom brought in fresh ones, and when the Cossack went into the backyard for a moment, Albina bent under the seat and asked her husband how he felt and whether he needed anything.

"I feel wonderful, and I do not need anything. I can easily lie down like this for another two days and two nights."

At night they came to a large village called Dergachi. So that her husband could climb out and stretch and get some fresh air, Albina did not stop at the horse station, but rather at a simple village inn. She gave some money to the Cossack to buy eggs and milk. The carriage stood under a roof and it was dark in the backyard, leaving Ludviga to stand guard, while Albina let her husband out of the carriage and gave him some food. Before the Cossack returned, Joe climbed back into his secret hiding place. Then they asked for new horses and continued on their way.

Albina felt her spirits rising higher and higher; she could not contain her joy and delight. There was no one to speak to except Ludviga, the Cossack, and their dog Tresorka, whom Albina played with constantly to amuse herself.

Ludviga, despite her ugliness, always suspected that every man she met was making advances to her, and now she suspected the same of this huge kindhearted Russian Cossack from the Urals who accompanied them. He looked at them with exceptionally kind light-blue eyes, and his simplicity and tenderness were attractive to both women. Besides Tresorka, at whom Albina shook her finger, not allowing the dog to smell under the seat, she was also entertained by Ludviga's comic flirting with the Cossack, who did not even suspect that it was directed toward him and kindly smiled at everybody. Albina was excited by danger, by their imminent success, by the wonderful weather, and by the fresh air, and she had a feeling she had not experienced for a very long time—the feeling of youthful joy and happiness. Fighting his physical discomfort (he felt very hot and thirsty), Migursky heard her merry conversation and forgot about himself, rejoicing when he heard the joyful voice of his wife.

By the end of the second day, something began to take shape in the fog. It was Saratov and the Volga River. With his sharp steppe eyesight, the Cossack could already see the Volga and the masts of the ships, and he pointed them out to Ludviga, who replied that she could see them also. Albina could make nothing out, but she said very loudly, so that her husband could hear, "This is Saratov, on the Volga River." And, as if addressing Tresorka, Albina described to her husband everything she could see.

XI

Instead of entering Saratov, Albina stopped for the night on the left bank of the Volga, at the Pokrovsky suburb, across from the city proper. She hoped that here, during the night, she would have time to talk to her husband and even to take him from the box for a while. But the Cossack, during that whole short spring night, never left the carriage but sat near it in an empty village cart in the inn yard. Ludviga sat in the carriage, as Albina had ordered her, and convinced that the Cossack did not move away from the carriage because of her, she winked at him, giggling and hiding her pockmarked face in her kerchief. But Albina saw nothing funny in this; she became more and more worried, unable to understand why the Cossack stayed next to the carriage all the time.

Several times during this very short night in May, with the dawn coming up in the sky almost instantly after sundown, Albina went through the stinking corridor leading to the backyard and out onto the porch of the small inn. But the Cossack did not sleep. With both feet hanging in the air, he still sat in the cart next to the carriage. Only early before dawn, when the roosters awoke and started to call to each other from one backyard to another, did Albina find a chance to approach her husband. The Cossack snored, lying comfortably in the cart. She quietly and cautiously approached the carriage and leaned closer to the box.

"Joe!" There was no answer. "Joe, Joe!" she said, louder, with some fear in her voice.

"What is it, my darling? What?" Migursky said sleepily from the box.

"Why didn't you answer?"

"I was asleep," he said, and from his voice she understood that he was smiling. "Should I get out?" he asked.

"No, you cannot. The Cossack is here," she said, and looked at the Cossack sleeping in the cart.

And it was strange: even though the Cossack snored, his eyes, his kind light-blue eyes, were open. Only when their glances met did he close his eyes.

Am I just imagining things, or was he not asleep after all? Albina asked herself. *It was probably my imagination,* she thought, and then addressed her husband again. "Just be patient a little longer. Would you like some food?"

"No, I would like to have a smoke."

Albina looked at the Cossack again. He seemed to be sleeping. *Yes, it must have been my imagination,* she thought. "It is time for me to go to the governor."

"All right. Good luck."

Albina took her best dress from her traveling chest and went to her room to change. After dressing, she crossed the Volga in a ferry. At the port, she took a cab to the governor, who received her in his office. He was an old man who wanted to look younger, and he liked this nice-looking Polish widow who spoke excellent French. He gave permission for everything she asked and invited her to see him again tomorrow to get a letter to the chief of the local police in Tsaritsyn. Albina was pleased that her visit had been successful and that her attractiveness had impressed the governor, as she had noticed from his manners. She was happy and full of hope as she sat in a small carriage on her way back, moving along the unpaved street that led down the hill to the city port.

The sun rose above the forest, and its slanting rays played on the surface of the rippled water, covering the wide river with silver. Up on the mountain, both to the right and to the left, she saw apple trees covered with blossoms; they looked like a white cloud and gave a wonderful smell. The multitude of boat masts along the bank of the river looked like a forest, and the wind-filled sails looked lovely against the slightly rough water of the huge river. In the port, she asked her groom whether it was possible to hire a boat to Astrakhan, and dozens of noisy, boisterous boat owners surrounded her, offering their services. She chose one of the boat owners whose face she liked more than that of the others and went to look at his boat, a rather narrow one that stood among the other boats in the crowded marina. The boat had a small mast with a sail, to make use of the wind, and if there were no wind, the boat had two oars, and two strong and merry sailors were sitting in the sun on the deck. The kind river pilot advised her not to leave the carriage, but rather to remove its wheels and put it on the boat, making the boat more stable so that they could sit more comfortably.

"May God give us good weather, and in five days or so we will be in the city of Astrakhan," he said.

Albina agreed to a price with the boat owner and asked him to come to the Loginov Inn in Pokrovsky to have a better look at the carriage and receive some advance money. Everything was working out even better than she had expected. Exultantly, Albina crossed the Volga, paid the ferryman, and went to the inn.

XII

Cossack Danilo Lifanov was from the village of Streletsk in Big Surt County. Thirty-four years old, he was serving his last month in the Cossack army. His family included a ninety-year-old grandfather who remembered the Pugachev rebellion, two brothers, and a sister-in-law, the wife of the elder brother, who had been sent to Siberia for his views as an Old Believer. He also had a wife, two daughters, and two sons. His father had been killed during the war with Napoleon, and Danilo Lifanov was the head of the family, the oldest man in the house. They had sixteen horses, two pairs of oxen, and fifteen hectares of their own plowed land on which they grew wheat. Danilo had served in the Orenburg Region, then in Kazan City, and now the term of his army service was coming to an end. He was firm in his old Christian faith: he did not smoke, he did not drink alcohol, he did not eat from the same dishes with other people who did not belong to his faith, and he strictly upheld his military oath. He was very deliberate and thorough in everything he did, and when he was handed orders from commanders, he put all his effort into fulfilling them, never for a minute forgetting to follow any order to the best of his understanding and ability.

Now his orders were to accompany two Polish ladies with two small coffins to Saratov, in order to protect them along the way from robbers, and to ensure that they behaved properly and did nothing strange. In Saratov he was to pass them on to the local officials, as had been arranged. So he brought them to Saratov, along with their small dog and their coffins. The women were quiet and tender, and although they were Polish women, they did nothing wrong. But there in the Pokrovsky suburb, in the evening, when he passed near the carriage he noticed that the dog jumped inside of the carriage, barked quietly a couple of times, and wagged its tail, and it seemed to him that someone's voice came from under the seat of the carriage. One of the Polish women, the older one, caught the little dog and carried it away, as if she were afraid of something.

There is something wrong here, the Cossack thought, and he started to watch more attentively. At night, when the young Polish woman came to the carriage, he pretended to be sleeping. He very clearly heard a man's voice from the box. Early that morning, he went to the police station and made an official statement: Things were not what they appeared to be. The Polish women were not traveling by themselves, and instead of dead bodies, they were transporting a living man in the box.

When Albina arrived at the inn, she was still enthusiastic and cheerful, convinced that their troubles were over and that in several days they would be free. She was surprised to see a fancy carriage with three luxurious horses and two Cossacks waiting next to them. People were crowded around the gates, trying to see into the yard.

She was so full of hope and energy that it did not at first occur to her that these horses and the crowd of people had some connection to her. She went into the yard, and as soon as she saw her carriage she understood the reason for the crowd, and she heard the desperate barking of Tresorka.

The most terrible of all possible things had happened. In front of the carriage stood a man with dark whiskers, issuing orders in a strong, hoarse, imperative voice. He wore an extremely clean official military uniform, with brass buttons shining in the sun, an impeccable military insignia on his shoulders, and clean, brightly polished tall boots.

Before him, between two soldiers, stood her Joe, still in peasant dress, with several straws in his tangled hair, and apparently not quite understanding what was happening, he kept shrugging his strong shoulders. Tresorka, unaware that he was the reason for this misfortune, showed his teeth and barked uselessly with great animosity at the police officer. When Migursky saw Albina, he trembled and tried to go to her, but the two soldiers held him back.

"It's nothing," said Migursky, with his kind, humble smile. "Don't worry, Albina."

"And here comes the dear lady herself!" said the police officer. "Please, come here, my dear. So these are the coffins of your children? Then who is this?" he said, winking at Migursky.

Albina did not answer. She only held both hands against her bosom, opened her mouth, and looked with horror at her husband.

As often happens at decisive moments in one's life—for example, just before death—Albina all at once felt a multitude of emotions and thoughts, while at the same time not quite believing in the reality of her misfortune.

Her first emotion was something she had felt for a long time—an upswelling of pride in her hero, her husband, who had been so abused and oppressed by these wild and rude people who still held him in bondage. How dare they keep *him*, the best of all people, at their mercy?

The second feeling that swept over her was the acknowledgment of the misfortune that had now befallen her. This realization brought back the memory of the great tragedy of her life, the death of her children. Again she asked, *Why? Why did it happen? Why were my children taken from me?* And that question led to another question: *Why? Why must he suffer, my most beloved man, my husband?* Suddenly she remembered the shameful punishment that awaited him, and that she and only she was guilty.

"Who is this man? Is he your husband?" the police officer asked again.

"Why? Why did this happen?" she cried, laughing hysterically, and then she fell onto the box, which had been taken down from the back of the carriage and placed on the ground.

Ludviga came to her, trembling, sobbing, her face covered with tears. "My dear lady, my dear lady! We should love God, and then nothing bad will happen, nothing," she said, touching Albina with her hand, uselessly trying to comfort her.

They handcuffed Migursky and led him from the yard. When Albina saw this, she ran after him, crying, "Forgive me, please forgive me! It's all my fault! It is me who is to blame!"

"They will see who is to blame, and they will take care of everyone—including you," said the police officer, holding her back with his hand.

Migursky was brought to the ferry, and Albina, without understanding what she was doing, followed him, not listening to Ludviga, who tried to calm her down.

While all this had been taking place, Cossack Danilo Lifanov had stood near the wheels of the carriage, looking alternately at the police officer and Albina. When Migursky was taken away, the little dog, Tresorka, came to him, wagging his tail as a dog usually does. He had gotten used to this man during their travel. Suddenly the Cossack moved away from the carriage. He took off his hat and threw it to the ground with all his strength, then he kicked the dog out of his way and went to the local pub. In the pub he asked for vodka, and he drank all day and all night, spending all his money and even pawning his clothes to drink some more. It was only the next night when he woke up drunk, lying in the gutter, that he finally stopped thinking about the question that had been torturing him: Had he done the right thing in reporting to the police that the Polish woman's husband was hidden in the box?

❧

Migursky was taken to court. For his attempt to escape, he was sentenced to a thousand hits by sticks. His family and Vanda, who had some connections in St. Petersburg, obtained a less severe punishment for him, and instead he was sent to permanent exile in Siberia. Albina followed him there.

Nikolai Pavlovich, the Tsar, was happy that he had suppressed the hydra of the revolution, not only in Poland, but everywhere in Europe. He was proud that he had carried on the tradition of Russian Tsarism, and that he had kept Poland under Russian power for the further benefit of the Russian people. And all the decorated military personnel, whose uniforms were covered with gold, praised him for what he sincerely believed himself to be—a great man, whose life was a great gift to humanity, and especially to the Russian people, even though, in reality, all his energy was directed toward making the Russian people even more corrupt and stupid, without understanding this himself.

DIVINE
AND
HUMAN

Divine and Human

I

It was the 1870s, in Russia, at the height of the struggle between the Tsarist government and the revolutionaries.

The general-governor of one of the southern provinces was a huge German with a great drooping mustache and cold eyes set in an expressionless face. His military uniform displayed a white cross at the neck. He sat one night in his office, at a table with four candles burning in shadowy green lamps, looking through and signing the papers his office manager had left for him. He would write on each his lengthy signature, "General Such-and-such," and put it aside.

Included among the papers was a document sentencing Anatoly Svetlogub, a student at the University of Novorossiisk, to death by hanging for participation in a conspiracy to overthrow the existing government. The general frowned particularly as he signed this paper. With aristocratic white fingers wrinkled by age and soap, he neatly lined up the edges of the pile of paper and put it aside.

The next paper was about the sums of money allocated for the transportation of food supplies. He read it attentively, considering whether they had calculated the amounts properly, and then he suddenly remembered a conversation with his deputy about this Svetlogub case. The general had argued that the explosives found at Svetlogub's apartment did not prove criminal intention. His deputy had insisted that, besides the dynamite, there was other evidence proving that Svetlogub was the leader of this gang. The general became lost in his thoughts, and his heart thudded nervously under his heavily decorated, firm, thick cotton uniform so that he could hardly breathe, and the white cross, his pride and joy, heaved up and down on his chest.

Maybe it's still possible to call back the head clerk and, if not repeal, at least suspend this sentence. Should I call him back, or not?

His heart beat harder. He rang the bell. His courier entered quickly and silently.

"Has Ivan Matveevich left?"

"No, your excellency. He's just gone into his office."

The general's heart skipped, then beat more rapidly, reminding him of the warning of the doctor who had listened to his heart a few days ago. "The most important thing is," the doctor had said, "as soon as you feel your heart, stop your work and try to entertain yourself. The worst thing is to be troubled too much. Do not allow this—ever."

"Shall I call for him?"

"No, it's not necessary," said the general.

Yes, thought the general, *indecisiveness agitates me the most. I signed the document, and that's the end of it. Ein jeder macht sein Bett und melss dar auf schlafen,** as the Germans say,* he thought, repeating his favorite proverb. *And this doesn't directly concern me. I am just following orders, and I should be above these considerations.* He pulled his eyebrows together into a frown, trying to inspire an attitude of alienated cruelty that didn't exist in his heart.

And then he remembered his last meeting with the Tsar, when the Tsar had made a very stern face, stared at him with glassy eyes, and said, "I have big hopes for you. You never pitied yourself during the war, and now, likewise, you will be very resolute in fighting the Reds. You will not allow yourself to be deceived nor

---

*One makes his bed, and one has to sleep in it.

frightened. Goodbye!" And then the Tsar had embraced him and offered his right shoulder to be kissed.

The general remembered this, and he remembered his answer to the Tsar: "I have only one desire—to dedicate my life to the service of my Tsar and my motherland."

When he remembered the feeling of servile affection that he derived from his unconditional devotion to his Tsar, he drove away his momentary hesitation, signed the rest of the papers, and rang the bell again.

"Has tea been served?" he asked.

"They are serving tea now, your excellency."

"All right. You can go."

The general sighed deeply, massaged his chest above his heart, and walked with heavy steps across the freshly polished floor of the huge, empty hall toward the living room from which he could hear voices.

The general's wife had guests: the governor with his wife, the patriotic old princess, and the officer of the guard, who was the fiancé of the general's eldest daughter.

The general's wife, a dry, tight-lipped woman with a cold face, was sitting at the low table, which was set with a silver teapot on a small burner. She was speaking in a false, sad voice to the wife of the governor, a fat woman who tried to look younger, about her troubles and her concerns for her husband's health.

"Every day new reports reveal more conspiracies, or other bad news, and all this weighs on Basil. He should make a final decision."

"Oh, don't tell me about it!" said the princess. "*Je deviens féroce quand je pense à cette maudite engeance.*"*

"Oh, yes, yes, it's terrible! Can you imagine? He works twelve hours a day with his weak heart. I am so afraid." Seeing her husband enter, she changed the subject. "Oh, yes, you should listen to him. Barbini is a wonderful tenor," she said, smiling brightly at the

*I grow furious when I think about those dreadful people.

wife of the governor, speaking about the visiting singer as naturally as if they had been speaking about this the whole time.

The general's daughter, a pretty and plump young lady, sat together with her fiancé in the far corner of the living room, behind a Chinese screen. She stood and came with her fiancé to her father.

"Hello, my dear. I have not seen you today," said the general, kissing his daughter and shaking hands with her fiancé.

After greeting his guests, the general sat and began to speak with the governor about the latest news.

"No, no, we are not allowed to speak about business," the wife of the general interrupted. "And now look—here is Mr. Kop'ev. He will tell you something funny. Hello, Mr. Kop'ev!"

And the famous comedian told the latest joke, which set everyone laughing.

II

"No, this can't be, it just can't! Let me go!" Svetlogub's mother cried, trying to escape from the arms of a high school teacher, her son's friend, and a doctor who were trying to hold her back.

Svetlogub's mother was a middle-aged, attractive woman with graying curls and wrinkles that radiated from the corners of her eyes. Svetlogub's friend, the teacher, had heard that the death sentence was signed, and he had come to prepare her for the bad news. But as soon as he began to speak about her son, she guessed from the tone of his voice and his humble glance that what she had feared had happened.

They were in a small room in the best hotel in town.

"Why are you holding me? Let me go!" she screamed, trying to break free of the doctor's grip. An old friend of the family, he held her now with one hand by her thin elbow; with the other, he placed a glass of medicine on the coffee table. She was glad that someone was holding her because she felt that she had to do something, but she did not know what she would do, and she was afraid of herself.

"Calm down, please. Here, drink some valerian drops," said the doctor, giving her the small glass of murky liquid.

Suddenly, she became quiet and nearly doubled over; her head drooped to her hollow breast. She closed her eyes and collapsed onto the sofa, remembering how three months ago her son had parted from her with a mysterious and sad face. Then she remembered him as an eight-year-old boy in a velvet coat—barefoot, with long, curling, blond hair. *And this, this very boy, her boy, they would do this to him!* she thought.

She lurched up suddenly and pushed her way to the table, managing to escape the doctor's hands. But when she reached the door, she fell into the armchair again.

"And they say there is a God! How can God exist? And how can he allow this? Devil take him, this God!" she cried, becoming hysterical, laughing maniacally. "He will be hanged, he will be hanged! They will hang him, this boy who left everything, even his career, who gave all his money to other men, to his people—everything he had! He gave everything!" Previously, she had always reproached her son for this self-sacrifice, but now she spoke of it as a merit, as if he were already martyred. "And they will do this to him, they will do this to him! And you say that God exists!" she shouted.

"I do not say anything. I just ask you to drink this medicine."

"I do not want anything. Ha ha ha!" She was laughing and crying, filled with despair.

By nightfall, she had become so exhausted that she could neither speak nor cry. She only gazed straight ahead, haunted, crazy. The doctor gave her a morphine injection and she fell asleep.

Her sleep was dreamless, but her awakening was even more terrible. The worst of all was that people could be so cruel—not only police officers and those terrible generals with their cleanly shaven cheeks, but everyone: the young woman servant who came with a calm face to clean up the room, and the people in the next hotel room who got together and laughed about something, as if nothing had happened.

III

Svetlogub was in his second month of imprisonment, confined alone in a small cell, where he suffered greatly.

Since his childhood, Svetlogub had sensed the falsehood of the exclusive position he held as a rich person. Although he had tried to ignore this awareness, whenever he encountered the sufferings of the poor, and sometimes when he simply felt good and happy, he became ashamed and sorry for these people—peasants, old men, women, children—who were born poor and who grew up and died without knowing the joys and comforts he had, and who spent their whole lives in hard labor and in need. When he graduated from the university, to escape this discomfort and guilt, he started a school for the country children in his village—a model school. Then he established a cooperative shop and then a shelter for homeless people, old men and old women. But oddly, while doing these things, he felt even more shame than when he shared a luxurious dinner with his friends or bought an expensive riding horse. He felt that all this was wrong, that there was something bad, something morally dirty in it.

During one of these times when he was disappointed with his village activity, he went to Kiev to meet with one of his closest friends from the university. Three years after this meeting, his friend would be executed by a firing squad in the moat in front of the Kiev fortress. But in the meantime, this gifted but rather unbalanced and passionate young man, who was easily and enthusiastically involved in everything, introduced Svetlogub to a secret society. The purpose of this society was to enlighten people, to help them to understand their rights, to create educational circles for simple people in order to free them from the power of the landowners and the government. The conversations Svetlogub had with this man and with his friends clarified everything he had felt only vaguely before. He understood what he had to do. Maintaining his relationships with his new friends, he returned to his village and there pursued new activities. He became a schoolteacher himself; he started classes for the adults; he read books and pamphlets to them; he explained to the peasants the state of their existence. Additionally, he published illegal books and brochures for the peasants, and without taking from his mother he contributed everything he could to help create such centers in other villages.

In taking these steps, Svetlogub encountered two obstacles that he had not expected: first, most people were not only completely indifferent to what he preached but viewed him almost with disgust. (Only a few exceptional people understood him, and they were often people of dubious morals.) The other obstacle was the government. The school was forbidden. He and his friends were searched by the police, and their books and papers confiscated.

Svetlogub did not pay much attention to the first obstacle, the indifference of the people, because he was so infuriated by the second, the senseless and abusive oppression of the government. His friends involved in similar activity elsewhere felt the same, and as their sense of irritation against the government grew greater and greater, most of his circle decided to fight the government with violence and terrorism.

The leader of this circle was a certain Mr. Mezhenetsky, a man everyone believed to possess unshakeable willpower, unassailable logic, and complete dedication to the revolutionary cause. Svetlogub submitted himself to the leadership of this man, and with the same energy he had formerly dedicated to his village activity, he gave himself entirely to terrorism.

This was dangerous—but the danger attracted Svetlogub most of all. *Victory or martyrdom,* he told himself. *If it's martyrdom, then this martyrdom will also be a victory, but only in the future.* And the fire that had been sparked in him did not die out during his seven years of revolutionary terrorist activity, but burned stronger and stronger because it was encouraged by the love and respect of his fellow workers.

He didn't ascribe any importance to the fact that he gave almost all of the estate he had inherited from his father to this cause, and he considered it a trifle, that he labored and suffered for the sake of his activities. He was saddened only by the sorrow his activity caused his mother and a certain young lady, his mother's adopted daughter, who lived with her, and who loved him.

One day an unpleasant man, a fellow terrorist whom Svetlogub didn't much like and who was wanted by the police, asked him to hide some explosives in his apartment. Svetlogub had agreed without hesitation, simply because he disliked this man. But the next day, Svetlogub's apartment was searched and the explosives were found. Svetlogub refused to answer any questions about where and how he had found the explosives.

And with this, the martyrdom he had anticipated began in earnest. Lately, when so many of his friends had been executed, imprisoned, or exiled, and so many women abused, Svetlogub almost wanted to suffer. In the first minutes of his arrest and during his initial interrogations, he felt a certain excitement, almost like joy.

He felt it when they stripped him, when they searched him, when they took him to prison, and when they locked the iron door behind him. But then the days passed—one day, a second, a third. Then the first week passed, and the second, the third. And in his lonely single cell, dirty, damp, crawling with insects, he wearied of the solitude and forced leisure that was interrupted only by knocks on the walls from other inmate friends who passed along old news, good and bad, and at times by the interrogations of cold and alien people who tried to pin more blame upon him. Gradually his moral and physical strength deteriorated; he became depressed and wanted only one thing: some kind of end to this torturous state. His sadness deepened because he was unsure of his strength to resist. In fact, by the second month of his incarceration, he felt that he might tell the whole truth to the police just to win his freedom.

He was horrified by this weakness, and he hated and despised himself and became even more depressed.

The most terrible thing of all was that in his incarceration he regretted all the energies and joys of youth that he had so easily sacrificed when he was free, and that now seemed so charming to him. Because of this, he repented of his former beliefs and sometimes even of all his activities. He found himself thinking that he could have lived so well, so happily, in freedom, in the countryside or abroad, among people and friends whom he loved and who loved him. He could have married that young lady, or some other young lady, and have lived a simple, joyful, radiant life with her.

IV

During the second month of his incarceration, on one of those days which were all so terribly alike, as the prison guard made his regular round past Svetlogub's cell, he passed to Svetlogub a small book. It had a brown leather cover with a golden cross in the center. The officer said that the wife of the governor-general of the province had visited the prison, and that she had left New Testaments, which were to be distributed to the inmates. Svetlogub thanked him with a slight smile and put the little book on the night table, which was bolted firmly to the wall.

When the guard went away, Svetlogub knocked on the walls and passed the news to his friends that a guard had come, and that he hadn't brought any news, but had only left the New Testament. His neighbor answered that he had received the same thing.

After dinner, Svetlogub opened the small book, its pages stuck together by the dampness, and began to read. Svetlogub had never read the New Testament as a book before. Everything he knew about it, he had learned in high school theology lessons or from the readings of ministers and deacons in church.

Chapter one began: "The book of the generation of Jesus Christ, the son of David, the son of Abraham. Abraham begat

Isaac and Isaac begat Jacob, and Jacob begat Judas and his brethren," he read. "Zorobabel begat Abiud," he continued. It was exactly what he had expected: some kind of confusing, unnecessary nonsense. If he were not in prison, he would not have read even to the end of the page. Nevertheless, he continued, merely for the exercise of reading. He thought, *I am reading just like Gogol's Petrushka, a puppet.* He finished the first chapter about the virgin giving birth, and about the prophecy that a man would be born who would be given the name Emmanuel, meaning "God with us."

What kind of prophecy is this? he thought, and continued reading. He read the second chapter about the traveling star, and the third chapter about John who ate locusts, and the next about some devil who suggested that Christ perform some sort of gymnastic feat by jumping from a roof. All of this was so uninteresting to him that, despite the boredom of prison life, he was going to close the book and begin his daily evening routine of catching the fleas in his shirt. But after he had removed his shirt, he suddenly remembered a fifth-grade exam in which he had forgotten one of the Beatitudes, and the rosy-faced, curly haired priest had became so angry that he had given him an unsatisfactory mark. He could not remember which Beatitude it had been, so he read that part of the Gospels: "Blessed are they who are persecuted, for theirs is the kingdom of heaven." *Perhaps this can be applied to us,* he thought.

"Blessed are ye when men shall revile you and persecute you. Rejoice and be exceedingly glad, for so persecuted they the prophets." "Ye are the salt of the earth. When the salt loses its power, how can you make it salty? You can have no use for it but to throw it away." *Surely this one could not be applied to us,* he thought, and continued reading.

After he read the fifth chapter, he thought, *"Do not be angry, do not commit adultery, love your enemies"—oh yes, if everybody lived like this, we wouldn't need a revolution.* Reading further, he delved deeper and deeper into those places in the book that were understandable. The more he read, the more he concluded that something very important was being said in this book. It was something essential and simple and touching, something that, although he had never heard it before, was familiar and obvious to him.

"And he said to all, 'Whoever wants to follow me should forget about himself, take up his cross, and follow me, because he who wants to find his life will lose it, and he who loses his life for my sake will save it. For what good does it do a man to gain the whole world and lose his own soul?'"

"Yes, yes, this is true, this is very true!" he cried, with tears in his eyes. "This is the same thing I wanted to do! Yes, I wanted to do the same: to give up my soul—not to preserve it, but to give it. This is joy and life." *I did many things for fame among people,* he thought, *not for the acclaim of the crowd, but for a good reputation among those I loved and respected—Natasha, Dmitry Shelomov. But then I had doubts and worries and hesitations. I felt good only when I did those things that I knew were necessary in my soul, and I wanted to give of myself, to give everything.*

From that day on, Svetlogub spent most of his time reading and meditating upon what was said in that book. His reading took him away from the conditions in which he lived and focused his thoughts in a way he had never experienced before. He wondered why people did not live in the way described in this book. *It is not for only one person to live this way, but for everyone. Live like this, and there will be no sorrow, no poverty, but only joy. If only I were free again. Sooner or later, they will either let me go or send me to hard labor. It's all the same. I will live like this no matter where I am. It can be done—and we need to live according to this book. Not to live like this is madness.*

V

On one of those days when he was in such high and excited spirits, a prison officer came into his cell at an unusual time for a visit, and he asked whether Svetlogub felt well, and whether he needed anything. Svetlogub was surprised; he didn't understand what this change meant. He asked for cigarettes, expecting refusal. The officer said that he would bring some, and another guard actually did bring him the cigarettes and matches.

Maybe someone said something about me to the officials, thought Svetlogub. Smoking, he paced back and forth in his cell, pondering the meaning of this change.

They brought him to court the next day. In the court building, where he had been several times before, they did not interrogate him. Without looking at him, one of the judges rose from his chair, and all of the others stood up. Holding a paper in his hands, the judge began to read in a loud and unnaturally flat voice.

Svetlogub listened, watching the faces of the judges. None of them looked at him, and all of them wore an important and sad expression.

In this paper it was written that Anatoly Svetlogub had participated in revolutionary activities, that this had been proven, and that his purpose had been to overthrow, in the near or distant future, the existing government. Therefore he was stripped of all his rights and sentenced to death by hanging.

Svetlogub listened and understood the meaning of these words as the judge pronounced them. He noticed the absence of logic in the words "near or distant future," and in depriving a man who is sentenced to death of his rights. But he did not comprehend the meaning for him of the things being read.

Only after he was told that he could go, and the police officer led him outside, did he begin to understand what had been said.

"Something is wrong here, something is wrong. This is some kind of nonsense. This just can't be," he said to himself, sitting in the carriage that took him back to prison.

He felt such force of life in himself that he could not imagine his death. He could not connect his consciousness of "self" with the idea of death, that is, the negation of his "self."

In his cell, Svetlogub sat on the prison cot, closed his eyes, and tried to imagine for himself what awaited him. He was utterly unable to imagine that he would not exist, and he could not imagine that people wanted to kill him.

Me—a young, kind, happy man, loved by so many people. He remembered the love his mother, Natasha, and his friends had for him. *They're going to kill me, to hang me! Who would do this, and why? And then—what will happen when I no longer exist? It cannot be,* he said to himself.

Then the officer of the guard came. Svetlogub didn't hear him coming.

"Who is it? Is it you?" Svetlogub asked, without recognizing him. "Yes, it is you! When will it happen?"

"I cannot know," said the officer. He stood for a moment in silence, and then said, in a soft, tender voice, "Here is our priest. He would like—to say a few good words—to see you."

"No, I don't want anything! I don't want anything! Go away!" said Svetlogub.

"Don't you want to write anybody a letter? That is allowed," the officer said.

"Yes, yes, give me some paper. I will write."

The officer went away.

That must mean it will happen in the morning, thought Svetlogub. *They always do it this way. Tomorrow morning, I will cease to exist . . . No, this cannot happen, it must be a dream.*

Then the guard came, a real prison guard familiar to him, and he brought two pens, an ink holder, a package of postal paper, and several blue envelopes. He drew his stool near the table. Everything was real, and it was not a dream.

It's best not to think, not to think at all. Yes, I should write, I should write to my mother, Svetlogub thought, sat down, and immediately started writing.

"My dear, my darling!" he wrote, weeping. "Please forgive me for all the woe I have caused you. Whether it was wrong or not, I could not have done otherwise. I ask of you only one thing. Please forgive me."

I have already said that, he thought. *Well, anyway, there is no time to rewrite it.*

"Do not mourn for me," he wrote further. "A bit earlier, a bit later . . . isn't it the same? But I am not afraid, I do not regret the things I did. I could not have done otherwise. Only please forgive me. And do not blame either my comrades, or those who execute me. None of them could have behaved any differently. Forgive them. They know not what they do. I cannot say these words about myself, but they are in my soul, they lift me up and calm me. Forgive me, please. I kiss your dear wrinkled old hands!" Two tears, one after another, fell on the paper and were swallowed by it. "I cry, but not out of sorrow or fear, but out of deep emotion before the most important moment of my life, and also because I love you. Please, do not reproach my friends, but love them. Especially love Prokhorov, because he was the cause of my death. It brings such joy to love someone who, because he is guilty, you would rather reproach and hate. To love a person who is your enemy is a great joy. Please tell Natasha that her love was my joy and consolation. I never understood this clearly before, but I knew it somewhere deep in my soul. My life was easier knowing that she existed and that she loved me. Now I have said everything. Goodbye forever!"

He read over the letter and, when he read Prokhorov's name near the end, suddenly remembered that other people might read this letter, that they most likely would read it, and that this would mean death for Prokhorov.

"O my God, what have I done!" he cried, and he tore his letter into strips and carefully burnt them one after another on the lamp.

Then he sat down to write with a terrible sense of despair, but presently he felt himself grow calmer, almost joyful.

He took another sheet of paper and started writing. One after another, thoughts crowded into his head.

"My dear, my darling mother!" he wrote, and again his eyes were filled with tears, and he had to wipe them away with his sleeve, in order to see what he wrote. "I did not know myself before, I did not know the strength of my love for you, the gratitude that always lived in my heart! Now I know. And when I remember all our petty quarrels and all the rude words I said to you, I feel pained and ashamed, and I cannot understand how I could have done these things. Please forgive me, and remember only the good things, if there was any good in me.

"I am not afraid of death. To tell you the truth, I do not understand it, I do not believe in it. But if there is such a thing as death, annihilation, then does it really matter whether we die thirty years, or thirty minutes, earlier or later? And if there is no death, then it is really all the same, whether earlier or later."

Why have I become philosophical? he thought. *I should say those things that were in the other letter, something good at the end. Yes.*

"Do not reproach my friends, but love them, especially that person who was the unintentional cause of my death. Please kiss Natasha for me and tell her that I loved her always."

He folded the letter, put it into the envelope, sealed it, and set it on the bed. Then he sat with his hands on his knees, swallowing his tears.

He still didn't believe that he was to die. Several times he asked himself again whether he was dreaming, and then he would try to wake up. That thought was followed by another: *Maybe all of life in this world is a dream, and waking up from it is death. And if that is so, then maybe the consciousness of this life is only the awakening from the dream of a previous life, the details of which I do not remember. So maybe this life is not the beginning but only a new form of life. Now I will die and enter another new form of life.* He liked this thought. But he also understood that neither this thought, nor any other thought, could make him fearless in the face of death. At last he grew tired of thinking. His brain did not work anymore. He closed his eyes and lay for a long time without thinking.

So how will it be? What will happen? he remembered again. *Nothing? No, not nothing. Then—what?*

And it became suddenly clear to him that no living person could ever answer these questions.

Then why do I ask myself about this? Why? Really, why? Rather than asking these things, I need to live like I was when I wrote this letter. Because we were all sentenced to death, a long time ago, all of us, eternally—and yet we all live. And we live with joy only when . . . we love. Yes, when we love. When I wrote this letter, I was in love, and I felt good. And that's how we need to live. And it's possible to live like this, everywhere and always, in prison or free, now and tomorrow and till the very end.

He wanted to say something nice to someone. He knocked at the door, and when the guard looked into his cell, he asked him what time it was and whether the changing of the guard would be soon, but the guard said nothing. Then Svetlogub asked for a senior officer. The senior officer came and asked what he wanted.

"I just wrote a letter to my mother. Please give it to her," he said, and the tears came to his eyes when he thought of her.

The senior officer took the letter and promised to deliver it. He started to go, but Svetlogub stopped him.

"Listen to me. You are a kind man. Why do you work in such a difficult job?" he said, tenderly touching the man's sleeve.

The officer of the guard smiled at him with unusual compassion and, lowering his eyes, said, "But one must make his living somehow."

"Leave this job. You could always find another place to work. You are such a kind person. Maybe I could do something . . ." The officer made a sobbing sound, turned quickly, and went out, closing the door behind him with a crash.

The emotion of the officer touched Svetlogub and he tried to suppress tears of joy. He began pacing back and forth, feeling no fear but only an emotional state of mind that lifted him above the world.

The question of what would happen to him after death, to which he had tried to find the answer and couldn't, seemed resolved in his mind—and not by some affirmative, rational answer, but by the recognition of the true life that was in him.

And he remembered the words of the New Testament: "Truly, truly I say to you that unless a seed of grain falls into the earth and dies, it will stay there alone. But if it dies it will bring much fruit." *So I will fall to the earth. Yes, truly, truly,* he thought.

I had better go to sleep, he thought suddenly, *so that I will not weaken later.* He lay down on his cot, closed his eyes, and fell asleep at once.

He awoke at six o'clock in the morning from a fresh and joyful dream. In his dream, he had been climbing trees with a pretty girl with curly blond hair. The trees were filled with ripe, black, sweet cherries, and he picked these cherries, trying to put them into a big copper pan. But the cherries did not fall into this pan; instead, they fell on the ground, and some strange animals that looked like cats played with the cherries, throwing them up and then catching them. Watching them, the girl laughed so infectiously that Svetlogub also started to laugh in his dream, without knowing why. Suddenly the copper pan fell from the girl's hands. Svetlogub tried to catch it but he was too late and the bowl dropped, making a huge noise as it hit the branches and fell to the earth. And Svetlogub woke up smiling, still hearing the noise of the huge falling bowl. But the noise was the unlocking of the iron catches in the corridor. He could hear footsteps in the corridor, and the noise of the armory, and then he remembered everything. *Oh, if only I could fall asleep again!* Svetlogub thought, but it was already impossible. The steps came near his door. He could hear how the key sought the keyhole and then how the door creaked open.

The officer, the warden, and several guards entered.

Death? So what? I will go away. Yes, it is good. Everything is good, Svetlogub thought, feeling the return of the previous day's moving, solemn state of mind.

VI

In the same prison where Svetlogub was held, there was also incarcerated an old man who belonged to the religious sect of

the Old Believers. He had begun to have doubts about the leaders
of his church, and he was looking for the real and true faith. He
denied not only the Orthodox Church of Patriarch Nikon, but also
all the bishops since the time of Tsar Peter the Great, whom he
considered to be the Antichrist. He called the royal government
"the tobacco state," and he openly said everything on his mind,
denouncing the priests and civil servants, for which he was tried
and imprisoned and then transferred from one jail to another. That
he was not free but imprisoned, that he was mocked by the prison
guards, that his hands and feet were shackled, that he was derided
by his fellow prisoners, that all of them together with their chiefs
denounced God and cursed each other and defiled the image of
God within themselves—all of these things did not bother him.
He had seen it all before, when he was free. He knew it arose from
the fact that people had lost the true faith and had scattered in different directions, like blind puppies from their mother. But despite
all this, he knew that the true faith exists. He knew this because he
felt this faith in his heart. He searched everywhere for this faith,
and most of all he hoped to find it in the Revelation of St. John:

"The liar will tell lies, the dirty man will become dirtier, the
truthful man will open the truth, and the holy man will become
even holier. But I will come soon and bring all the punishments
with me to give everybody according to his deeds."

He read this mysterious book again and again, awaiting at
every moment "the future" that would give to everyone according
to his deeds and also reveal the divine truth to people.

On the morning of Svetlogub's execution, the old man heard
the drums and, climbing to his window, he saw through the prison
bars how the cart was brought, and how a young man emerged
from the prison with shining eyes and curly hair, and mounted the
cart with a smile. There was a book in the small white hand of this
young man. He pressed this book to his heart, and the Old
Believer recognized that this was a New Testament. Nodding and
smiling at the other prisoners in their windows, the young man

exchanged glances with the Old Believer. The horses started. The cart carrying this pale, angelic man, surrounded by prison guards, rattled on the paving stones as it drew away beyond the gates.

The Old Believer climbed down from his window, sat on his cot, and thought, *This man has found the truth. And the servants of Antichrist will take a rope and hang him so that he shall not reveal that truth to other people.*

VII

It was a gloomy autumn morning. One could not see the sun. A warm, damp breeze blew from the sea.

The fresh air, the city, houses, horses, people looking at him— all of this entertained Svetlogub. Sitting on the bench at the top of the cart with his back to the groom, he looked into the faces of the soldiers in the cart and the citizens who met him on the way.

It was early in the morning, and the streets along which they moved were almost empty. They encountered only working people, big masons with their clothes covered with drops of lime, who moved hurriedly out of the street, then stopped and turned back when the cart had passed. One of them said something and waved his hand, and they all turned and went back to their work. The tinkers who transported huge pieces of iron in their wagons stopped their horses, giving way to the cart, and gazed at him with puzzled curiosity. One of them took his hat off and crossed himself. A woman cook in her white apron and cap, with a small pan in her hand, came out through a gate, saw the cart, and quickly returned to her yard. She soon came back to the street with another woman, and both of them stared wide-eyed and out of breath at the cart and gazed after it for as long as they could see it. A shabbily dressed and unshaven old man, pointing at Svetlogub, was expressing his disapproval with animated gestures to the superintendent of a house. Racing to catch up with the cart, two boys ran next to it, their heads turned, not watching in front of them. One, the older boy, took long, fast steps. The other, small and hatless, held onto the hand of the older boy, and fearfully glancing at the cart, ran with quick little steps, his small feet stumbling all the time, trying to keep up with the elder boy. Meeting the younger boy's eyes, Svetlogub nodded his head. This gesture from a terrible man who was being transported in this cart embarrassed the little boy so much that his eyes grew wide, and he opened his mouth and was about to cry. Then Svetlogub kissed his hand and smiled kindly at him. The boy answered with an unexpected, wide, sweet smile.

During all of this, Svetlogub's acknowledgment of what awaited him did not destroy his peaceful, solemn mood.

It was only when the cart came to the gallows, only when he saw the pillar with the crossbeam and the rope gently swaying in the wind, that he felt as though he had received a physical blow to the heart. He suddenly felt dizzy and nauseated. But that did not last for long. Around the wooden structure he saw dark rows of soldiers with their rifles, and officers walking in front of the soldiers. As soon as he emerged from the cart, there came a sudden, sharp sound—the beat of the drums. It made him tremble. Behind the rows of soldiers, Svetlogub saw the carriages of gentlemen and ladies who had come to watch the event. All of this surprised Svetlogub at first, but then he remembered himself and the kind of person he had been before prison, and he pitied these people, and mourned that none of them knew what he knew now. *But they will find out. I will die, but the truth will not die. They will know the truth. And all of them—not I, who will be dead soon—but all of them can and will be happy.*

They brought him to the wooden platform, and an officer came up behind him. The drums stopped beating and the officer read, in an especially unnatural voice that sounded very weak in that wide open place after all the noise of the drums, that foolish death sentence. It was the same sentence that had been read to him in court—depriving the condemned man of his rights and all that business about the near or distant future. *Why, why are they doing all this?* thought Svetlogub. *What a pity that they do not know the things I have learned, and that I cannot pass them on. But they will find out. Everyone will find out.*

The same prison priest, a very thin man with long, thin hair, came to him wearing deep purple robes. He had one small golden cross on his bosom, and a second big silver cross clutched in a dry, weak, skinny white hand that protruded from his black velvet sleeves.

"Most merciful Lord," the priest intoned, moving the cross from his left hand to his right and holding it up to Svetlogub to kiss.

Svetlogub trembled and stepped aside. He almost swore at the priest who participated in this evil deed while speaking about mercy. Then he remembered the words of the New Testament: *They know not what they do.* So, with an effort, he said humbly, "Please excuse me, but I do not need this. Forgive me, please—I really don't need this! Thank you."

He held his hand out to the priest. The priest returned his cross to his left hand and shook Svetlogub's hand, trying not to look into his eyes; then he stepped down from the platform. The drums began to beat again, overpowering all other noises. After the priest left, a middle-aged man came to Svetlogub with fast, heavy steps that shook the platform. He had broad shoulders and muscular hands and wore a coat over the bulky shirt of a Russian peasant. This man looked Svetlogub over quickly and came so close that Svetlogub could smell the unpleasant odors of wine and sweat. The man's strong fingers grasped Svetlogub's hands above the wrists, brought them behind his back, and tied them very firmly to each other, so that Svetlogub could feel the pain. After he had bound Svetlogub's hands, the executioner stopped for a moment, as if pondering something, and looked absently at Svetlogub, then at the things he had brought up and placed on the platform, then at the rope hanging from the beam. When he had calculated what he needed to do, he walked to the rope, did something to it, and moved Svetlogub under the rope at the end of the platform.

When the death sentence had first been announced in the courtroom, Svetlogub had not comprehended the full meaning of those things that were told him; now he could not grasp the full meaning of the impending moment. He looked with astonishment at the executioner, hastily and deftly carrying out his terrible duty. The executioner's face was the simple face of a Russian working person—not evil, but concentrated on performing a necessary and complicated task as well as he could.

"Hey, you, move over there—well, would you please move this way," the man said hoarsely, pushing him toward the gallows. Svetlogub moved there.

"Oh, my God, please help me and save me!" he said.

Svetlogub didn't believe in God, and he had often laughed at those who did believe in God. Even now he didn't believe—he didn't believe because he could not put the idea of God into words or even embrace it in his thoughts. But now he understood something: that which he now addressed—he knew this for certain—was utterly real, the most real among all things he had ever known. And he knew that addressing God was necessary and important. He knew this because these words calmed and strengthened him at once.

Taking his place on the gallows, he saw the rows of soldiers and onlookers present at the execution and thought once again, *Why, why are they doing this?* And he pitied both himself and all of them, and tears appeared in his eyes.

"Don't you pity me?" he asked, catching the glance of the executioner's sharp gray eyes.

The executioner stopped for a second. An evil expression suddenly appeared on his face. "Stop this! Stop talking," he muttered, and stooped quickly down to the ground where his vest and a piece of cloth lay. He stood behind Svetlogub, and with one swift motion, he put a cotton sack over Svetlogub's head and pulled it hard and fast down to the middle of his back and his breast.

"Into your hands I deliver my spirit." Svetlogub remembered the words from the New Testament.

His spirit did not resist death, but his strong young body would not accept it.

He wanted to struggle, he wanted to cry, he wanted to jump, but at that moment he felt somebody push him. He lost his point of equilibrium—he felt the animal-like horror of suffocation, he heard a noise in his head, and then everything disappeared.

Svetlogub's body hung on the rope, swaying back and forth. His shoulders moved twice, up and down.

After waiting about two minutes, the executioner frowned grimly, put both hands on the shoulders of the dead body, and with a strong movement pressed it downwards. All movements of the corpse stopped except the slow sway of a hanging doll. The head moved unnaturally forward in the sack and the long legs hung in prisoners' socks.

The executioner descended from the platform and told the chief officer that the body could be removed from the noose and buried.

An hour later, the body was taken from the gallows and brought to the unconsecrated cemetery.

The executioner had wanted only to do his job. And his job was not easy. Svetlogub's words, "Don't you pity me?" would not leave his head. A former murderer, he was still a prisoner; becoming the executioner had provided him with some measure of freedom and more comfort. But from this day on, he refused to perform his job. Within a week he drank away not only all the money he had received from Svetlogub's execution, but all of his rather expensive wardrobe. Soon he was reduced to such a state that he was put in "the hole" in the prison. From "the hole," he was moved to the prison hospital.

VIII

One of the leaders of the revolutionary terrorist party, Ignaty Mezhenetsky, the same man who had invited Svetlogub into the terrorist movement, was transferred from the province where he had been arrested to St. Petersburg. The Old Believer who saw Svetlogub depart for execution was incarcerated in the same prison for a short period, awaiting removal to Siberia. As always, he pondered how and where he might find the true faith, and sometimes he remembered that bright and enlightened young man who went to his death smiling joyfully.

When he found out that a friend of this young man, a man of the same faith, sat in the same prison, the Old Believer was overjoyed, and he asked a prison guard to bring him to Svetlogub's friend.

Despite the strict prison discipline, Mezhenetsky had not lost contact with the people of his party, and every day he expected news from those who were excavating the tunnel Mezhenetsky had planned in order to put explosives under the Tsar's train. Now, recalling some details he had forgotten, he tried to think of a way to pass this information on to his friends. When the prison guard came to his cell and softly, carefully told him that another prisoner wished to see him, he was delighted because he thought this meeting could help him communicate with his party.

"And who is this man?" he asked.

"He is a peasant."

"And what does he want?"

"He wants to speak about faith."

Mezhenetsky smiled. "Tell him that I want to see him. Send him here," he said. *The Old Believers also hate the government*, he thought. *Maybe he can help me.*

The prison guard went away. Several minutes later, the door opened and a short, dry old man with thick hair, a thin gray triangle of beard, and very kind, tired blue eyes entered the cell.

"What do you want?" Mezhenetsky asked. The old man looked at him with his blue eyes and then slowly lowered them and offered him a small, dry, energetic hand.

"What do you want?" Mezhenetsky repeated.

"I wish to have a word with you."

"What word?"

"About faith."

"About which faith?"

"People say that you are from the same faith as that young man whom the servants of the Antichrist killed with a piece of rope in Odessa."

"Which young man?"

"The one who was killed in Odessa with a rope."

"Maybe Svetlogub?"

"Yes, that's him. Was he your friend?" With every question the man peered inquiringly with his kind eyes into Mezhenetsky's face and then lowered them again.

"Yes, this man was close to me."

"Are you from the same faith?"

"So it seems," said Mezhenetsky, smiling.

"That's what I want to talk to you about."

"What is it that you want?"

"I want to learn about your faith."

"Our faith? Then sit down," said Mezhenetsky, shrugging his shoulders. "Our faith is this: I believe that there are those who seized power and now they torture and deceive the people. I believe that we should not pity ourselves; rather, we should fight with those men in order to free our people from exploitation," said Mezhenetsky, as he had said many times before. "They torture people," he clarified, "and those men should be destroyed. They kill others, and we have to kill them in return, until they come to their senses."

The old man sighed several times without lifting his eyes.

"Our faith is that we should not feel sorry for ourselves, but that we should overthrow the despotic government and establish a free, elected government."

The old man sighed deeply. Then he stood up, straightened the flaps of his gown, and fell prostrate at Mezhenetsky's feet, striking his forehead on the dirty wooden boards of the floor.

"Why are you bowing?"

"Do not lie to me. Reveal to me what your faith is really about," said the man, without standing, without raising his head.

"I told you about our faith. But stand up, please—otherwise I won't say anything else."

The Old Believer stood. "Was this also the faith of that young man?" he asked, standing before Mezhenetsky and gazing into his face with his kind eyes, then lowering them.

"Yes, he had the same faith, and he was hanged for it. And now for the same faith I am taken to St. Peter-and-Paul's Fortress."

The old man bowed very low, and then silently left the cell.

No, that young man had a different faith, he thought. *That young man knew the true faith, and this one was either boasting that he is of the same faith, or he doesn't want to reveal it to me. So I will keep looking for the true faith, first here and then in Siberia. God is everywhere, and people are everywhere. If you are moving ahead and don't know how to go further, ask the way,* thought the old man. Again he picked up the New Testament, which opened by itself to Revelation. He put on his glasses, sat in front of the window, and began to read.

IX

Seven years passed, during which time Mezhenetsky was in solitary confinement in St. Peter-and-Paul's Fortress. Then he was sent to hard labor in Siberia.

He endured much during those seven years, but the direction of his thoughts did not change, nor did his energy lessen. During the interrogations before his imprisonment at the fortress, he surprised all the interrogating officers and judges with his hard, cold contempt of the people in whose power he remained. Deep in his soul he suffered, knowing he would never again be free, never be able to finish the business he had started, but he did not show this. When confronted with his enemies, he was filled with angry energy. When he was questioned, he remained silent and spoke only when he might mock his interrogators, whether police officers or prosecutors.

When he was told the usual phrase—"If you make a complete confession, you can make your situation easier"—he would give a derogatory smile and after a short silence reply, "If you think I would betray my friends out of fear or a desire to obtain some advantage for myself, then you judge me according to the standards of your own behavior. Do you really think that, in doing the things for which you judge me, I did not prepare for the worst? You can surprise me with nothing, and nothing can frighten me. Do anything you wish, anything you want, anything you can, but I will not speak."

And he was pleased to see that they looked at each other with embarrassment.

When he was placed in a small prison cell in St. Peter-and-Paul's Fortress, with only a tiny, darkened glass window set high in its damp walls, he understood that it was not for months, but for years. Then he experienced real fear. It was terrible to experience this deadly silence and understand that he was not alone here, that behind these walls were other prisoners like himself, sentenced for ten or twenty years—some who wanted to hang themselves, others who had gone mad or were slowly dying from tuberculosis. Here there were women, men, maybe his friends . . .

After many years, you will be as they are now: you will either go insane, or you will hang yourself, or you will simply die and nobody will find out about you, he thought.

Deep in his soul he felt animosity toward all people, but especially toward those who were the cause of his incarceration. And this hatred demanded objects of hatred; it needed some movement, some noise. Here there was only complete, deathly silence, the soft steps of silent people who did not answer his questions, the noise of opening and closing locks, food at the usual hour, visits by silent people, the dim light of the rising sun and then darkness and the same silence, the same very soft steps, the same sounds. It was the same today and tomorrow and again the next day, and the evil within him could not find an outlet, and it began to consume his heart.

He tried to knock on the door, on the walls. Nobody responded to him, nobody answered. After his knock, there came only the same quiet steps and then a queerly controlled voice threatening him with punishment in the hole.

The only time he found some relief was in sleep, but waking up was terrible. In dreams he always saw himself at liberty, and mostly engaged in things that normally he would have thought incompatible with revolution. Either he played an old, strange-looking violin, or he was womanizing, or he was riding in a boat or hunting or making some strange scientific or scholarly discovery for which he was named honorary Doctor of Philosophy at some foreign university and made a gracious speech at the reception dinner. His dreams were so bright and clear and reality so dull that he found that his memories became nearly indistinguishable from reality.

Only one thing was difficult in his dreams: he usually awoke just at the moment when something he had striven for, something he desired was about to happen. But suddenly there would be a push-push of his heart, and with one more push this lovely world vanished and only the unsatisfied, torturing desire remained, and he would again be surrounded by great gray walls covered with spots of dampness barely lit by the lamp, and under his body the stiff, rotten, lumpy pallet.

Even though sleep was the best time for him, the longer he spent in prison, the less he slept. He longed for sleep ardently, but the more he wanted it, the more excited he became, and then he could not fall asleep. As soon as he asked himself, *Am I falling asleep?* all his drowsiness disappeared, and he was awake.

When he ran or jumped for exercise in his cave, it did not help. The increased activity made him feel even weaker and excited his nerves even more. It also caused a pain at the back of his head, and if he closed his eyes he saw, against a painfully bright background, terrible faces covered with fur or completely bald, or with huge, curved mouths, each one more horrifying than the last. These faces grimaced at him; then they began to appear before him even when his eyes were open, not only faces but whole figures, and they started to talk and dance in front of him. Frightened, he jumped up with a start, hitting his head against the wall and crying out.

A small hole in the door opened. "You are not allowed to make noise," said a calm and even voice.

"I want an interrogator!" yelled Mezhenetsky.

No one answered him, and the opening closed.

And he felt so desperate that he wanted only one thing: death.

One day when he felt this way, he decided to take his own life. There was a ventilation grate in the cell to which he could attach a rope, and by stepping off the prison bed he would be able to hang himself. He had no rope, so he tore his sheet into narrow strips—but there were not enough of these strips. Then he decided to die from hunger, and he did not eat for two days. On the third day, when he was very weak, the hallucinations returned with greater force. When food was brought to him, he was found lying on the floor, unconscious, with his eyes open.

The doctor came to his cell; he put Mezhenetsky on the bed and gave him bromide and morphine, and Mezhenetsky fell asleep.

When he woke up the next day, he saw the doctor standing beside him, shaking his head. Suddenly, Mezhenetsky was seized by that familiar, invigorating feeling of anger that he had not experienced for a long time.

"You should be ashamed," he said to the doctor, who was bending over him to take his pulse. "You should be ashamed to work here! You treat me only in order to torture me afterwards. You might as well perform an operation, finish it, and then immediately start a new operation on the same patient."

"Please lie on your back," said the doctor without emotion, without looking at him, removing his stethoscope from his side pocket.

"People like you cured the wounds of the punished man so that he could receive the rest of his five thousand lashes. May the devil take you! Go to hell!" Mezhenetsky yelled, sliding his legs off the bed. "Get away! Get out of here! I *want* to die!"

"That will do no good, young man. You are very rude, but we have our own responses to rudeness."

"Go to hell! Go to hell!"

Mezhenetsky looked so terrible that the doctor hurried out of the cell.

X

Either the medicine helped, or Mezhenetsky had lived through his crisis. Or perhaps his rising anger toward the doctor had cured him. After that episode, he took hold of himself again and started a completely new life.

They cannot keep me here eternally, and they will not, he thought. *They will release me one day. Perhaps—and what is most likely—there will be a new regime (since my friends keep working for our cause), so I must stay alive so that I can come out full of energy, healthy and able to continue our work.*

He thought for a long time about the best way to live to achieve this purpose, and decided to follow this plan: He went to bed at nine o'clock, forcing himself to lie down—either to sleep or not to sleep, it was all the same—until five o'clock in the morning. At five o'clock he got up, washed himself, did morning exercises and then, as he said, went to do some errands. In his imagination he went around St. Petersburg, from Nevsky Prospect to Nadezhdinskaya Street. He imagined anything he might experience on this walk: the shop signs, the houses, the police officers, the carriages, and the pedestrians. Then he visited the house of his friend and comrade, and they met with other friends and discussed their plans for the future, sometimes having heated arguments. Mezhenetsky spoke for himself and for the others. Sometimes he spoke so loudly that the prison guard reprimanded him from the small window in the door, but Mezhenetsky ignored this and continued his imaginary day in St. Petersburg. After two or three hours spent with his friends, he came back home and enjoyed his dinner, first in his imagination and then in reality, but he always ate with moderation. Then, in his imagination, he spent the rest of his day at home and worked either on history or on mathematics—and sometimes, on Sundays, on literature. His study of history consisted of reciting the facts and chronology of some epoch and people. In his mathematics lesson, he would recall various theorems and equations, or try to solve geometrical puzzles (he enjoyed this most of all). On Sundays, he would recall the works of writers—Pushkin, Gogol, Shakespeare—and sometimes he composed his own.

Before going to bed, he made one more small tour: in his imagination, he had joking, lively, but sometimes serious conversations with his friends, both men and women. Sometimes he recreated past conversations, and sometimes he created new ones. Before going to bed, he took two thousand real steps in his cage for exercise, and then he lay down on his prison bed. Most nights, he fell asleep.

The next day would be the same. Sometimes he traveled to the south and spoke to the people, started a rebellion, and after a successful fight against the landlords, he gave the land to the peasants. This all took place in his mind—not all at once, but slowly and in fine detail. In his imagination, his revolutionary party won every time, and the government became weak and had to call a parliamentary election. The Tsar's family and all the persecutors and oppressors of the working people disappeared, and then there was a republic, and Mezhenetsky was elected president. Sometimes he arrived at this final outcome too quickly, and then he would start again from the beginning and reach that goal by some other means.

He went like this for a year, or two or three—sometimes he deviated from this strict way of life, but mostly returned to it. As he guided his imagination, his hallucinations and terrible night-mares disappeared. Only occasionally did he have sleepless nights when those hallucinations with the terrible, grotesque faces returned, when he would dream that he looked at the ventilation grate and got a rope, made a loop, and hanged himself. But these fits of madness did not last long, and he could overcome them.

So he lived for almost seven years. When that phase of his incarceration ended and he was to be taken to a labor camp in Siberia, he emerged from St. Peter-and-Paul's Fortress fresh, healthy, and in full possession of his mental faculties.

XI

He was transported to Siberia as a very important criminal, alone and incommunicado. It was not until he was placed in Krasnoyarsk Prison that he could communicate with other political criminals who had also been brought there for hard labor. There were six of them, two women and four men. They were young people, his followers, revolutionaries of the next generation, those who had come along behind him. Mezhenetsky did not know them, but he was very interested in them. Mezhenetsky was expecting them to be people who followed his ideas and therefore highly respected everything that had been done by their predecessors, especially him, Mezhenetsky. He was prepared to treat them in an affectionate, condescending manner. It was an unpleasant surprise that these young people not only did not recognize him as their predecessor and teacher, but treated him as if *they* were superior, and looked down on his old-fashioned views. According to these new revolutionaries, everything Mezhenetsky and his friends had done, all their efforts to incite a rebellion among the peasants, and more importantly all their terrorist assassinations—General-Governor Kropotkin, General Mezentsev, the head of police, and even Alexander II himself—all these had been so many mistakes. These young people were the product of the conservative period that flourished under the rule of Alexander III and which brought society backwards, almost back to the spirit of serfdom. And according to their views, the path to liberation of the people was completely different.

For nearly two days and two nights, Mezhenetsky debated, almost without interruption, with his new acquaintances, especially with their leader, Roman, who was called only by his first name. Roman's unwavering confidence that he was right, and his condescending, even mocking negation of all that had been accomplished previously by Mezhenetsky and his friends, deeply pained Mezhenetsky.

Roman maintained that the simple folk are a very stupid crowd—"a herd"—and that it is impossible to do anything with people who are in that stage of development. All efforts to start rebellion among the country population in Russia would be about as effective as trying to burn stone or ice. You have to educate people, to bring them to solidarity, and only big industry and socialist organizations can do that. He recited statistics and the opinions of authorities from memory. Land makes people conservative; they become its slaves, not only in Russia but also in all of Europe. People should be freed from the land, and the faster this is done the better. The more people go to factories, and the more land the capitalists take, and the more people are oppressed, the better. Despotism, and more importantly capitalism, can only be destroyed by solidarity of the people. This solidarity can be achieved only through trade unions of workers—in other words, when the masses stop being landowners and become proletarians.

Mezhenetsky argued with Roman, becoming very heated. He was especially irritated by a nice-looking brunette with very dark, shining eyes. She sat at the window as if she were not participating in their conversation, but she sometimes inserted a few words that supported Roman's arguments, or looked up with some disdain at Mezhenetsky's words.

"Can you change all the people from peasants to factory workers?" Mezhenetsky said.

"Why not?" Roman said. "This is a general economic law."

"How do we know that this law is universal?" Mezhenetsky asked.

"Read Kautsky," smiled the dark brunette woman with contempt.

"And if we accept," Mezhenetsky said, "although I do not accept it, that the people will all become proletarian and factory workers, why do you think this will take shape in the way you have determined beforehand?"

"Because it has been proven by science," said the brunette, turning from the window.

When they spoke about the means necessary to reach their goal, their differences became even more pronounced. Roman and his friends believed that it was necessary to prepare an army of workers by promoting the transition from peasants to factory workers and educating them about socialism. But they would not fight the government openly. Mezhenetsky argued that it was necessary to battle the government directly and to use terrorism because the government is stronger and smarter.

"You will not deceive the government, but they you. We, too, propagandized the people—but we also fought the government."

"And you achieved so much!" the brunette said sarcastically.

"Fighting openly with the government is a waste of energy," Roman said.

"The first of March* was a waste of energy?" Mezhenetsky yelled. "We gave our lives! Instead, you sit quietly at home, enjoying life and merely preaching!"

"We are not enjoying life very much," Roman said, looking at his friends and laughing loudly and self-confidently.

The brunette shook her head and smiled scornfully at Mezhenetsky.

"We do not enjoy life very much," Roman said. "And if we sit here, it is because of the reactionary regime in this country which was created by the first of March."

---

*The date of the assassination of Russian Tsar Alexander II.

Mezhenetsky grew silent. He felt like he was being suffocated by anger, and he went out into the corridor.

XII

Mezhenetsky tried to calm himself by walking up and down the corridor. Because it was just before evening roll call, the doors of the prison cells were open. A tall prisoner with half of his head shaved,* a blond beard, and a kind face approached Mezhenetsky. "There is another prisoner in our cell who saw you, and he said, 'Please bring him to me.'"

"Which prisoner?"

"They call him 'Tobacco-State'—that is his nickname. He is an old man, from the Old Believers. He said 'bring this man to me.' He was talking about you, sir."

"Where is he?"

"Here, in our cell," the new convict with the half-shaven head said. "He asked me to call you." Mezhenetsky accompanied the man to a small cell with beds for several prisoners, where they lay or sat.

The Old Believer lay under a gray prison gown at the end of the bare bed; it was the same old man who had come to Mezhenetsky seven years before to ask about Svetlogub. The face of the old man was pale, completely dried out and wrinkled, but his hair was as thick as before. His thin beard was completely gray and stuck upward. He had the same blue eyes, still as kind and attentive. He lay on his back, and it seemed that he had a fever. There was an ill red flush on his cheeks.

Mezhenetsky approached him. "What do you want?" he asked.

The old man lifted himself up on an elbow and offered Mezhenetsky a dry, small, trembling hand to shake. He tried to say something, then tried with difficulty to take a breath. Finally,

---

*At the time of their arrival at prison, the heads of new convicts were half-shaved.

breathing heavily, he said quietly, "You did not tell me the truth that time, but God be with you, I am telling the truth to everybody."

"What truth are you telling?"

"I am telling about the lamb … the lamb, the truth … That young man was with the lamb. It is said that the lamb will have victory over everybody … and those who are with him, they are the chosen and the faithful."

"I do not understand," Mezhenetsky said.

"You should understand being in spirit. The kings will have power, and they will be allied with the evil beast. But an innocent lamb will defeat them."

"Which kings?" Mezhenetsky asked.

"There are seven kings. Five of them fell, one remained, and one will come in the future but hasn't come yet. And when he comes, there will be very little time for him to stay in power—and then the end will come for him as well. Do you understand?"

Mezhenetsky shook his head, thinking that the old man was so feverish his words had no meaning.

The other prisoners, his cell mates, thought the same thing: The shaved prisoner who had called Mezhenetsky gently elbowed him to get his attention, winked at the old man, and said, "He talks and talks, our 'Tobacco-State.' He speaks but doesn't know what he says."

Most people, looking at the old man, agreed with Mezhenetsky and his cell mate. But the old man knew very well what he said, and the words he spoke had very clear and deep meaning for him. They meant that the evil one would not remain in power for long, that the lamb would conquer the world with kindness and humility and then wipe away all tears, and there would be no crying, no illness, no death. He felt that this would soon come throughout the world because it had already come in his soul, which, being very close to death, was becoming enlightened.

"Behold, it is coming soon! Amen! Come, Lord Jesus!" he said, and he looked up and smiled slightly to Mezhenetsky, and it seemed to Mezhenetsky that it was the smile of a madman.

XIII

Here he is, *the representative of the people*, thought Mezhenetsky, leaving the old man's cell, *and he is the best of them. Yet he is in such darkness!* Remembering Roman and his friends, he thought, *They say that with such people as he is, you can do nothing.*

For some time Mezhenetsky had worked among simple people as a revolutionary, and he had come to know, as he would say, the great inertia of the Russian peasant. He had met soldiers and veterans, and he knew that they were completely faithful to their oath to the Tsar, completely obedient, and it was impossible to persuade them to change their views simply by talking to them. Though he knew all this, he had not acted upon the conclusions he had drawn from this knowledge.

His conversation with the new revolutionaries had upset him. They had claimed that everything that had been done by Halturin, Kibalchich, and Perovskaya* had been useless, even harmful, and it had resulted in the reactionary period of Alexander III. Due to these men and women the Russian people were convinced that all revolutionary activity was initiated by the landlords, who had killed the Tsar because the Tsar freed their slaves and serfs.

This is so stupid! Such a huge misunderstanding! he thought, while pacing in the corridor.

All the cell doors were now closed except that of the new revolutionaries. Approaching their cell, Mezhenetsky heard the voice of the brunette he hated and the loud, decisive voice of Roman. They were evidently talking about him. He stopped to listen.

Roman said, "Without considering economic laws, they didn't understand what they were reforming, and that was their mistake ..."

Mezhenetsky could not listen to the end. He did not want to know what Roman thought he should do. Roman's tone alone demonstrated the complete disregard and hatred those people felt

---

*Famous Russian terrorists and revolutionaries.

for him, for Mezhenetsky, the hero of the revolution, who had given twelve years of his life for this purpose.

And a terrible feeling of anger, such as he had never experienced before, rose up in Mezhenetsky. He hated everyone and everything, this entire senseless world. In this world, only those who were like animals could survive: that old man with his lamb; those half-animal, half-people executioners and guards; and those creeping, self-confident, half-dead conservative revolutionaries, like Roman and his friends.

The guard came to take the women prisoners to the women's part of the prison. Mezhenetsky went to the furthest end of the corridor to avoid them. When the prison guard came back, he locked the cell door of the new political prisoners and asked Mezhenetsky to go to his cell. Mezhenetsky did so but he asked him not to lock the door.

In his cell, he lay down on his bed with his face to the wall.

Is it true that I spent all my force, all my energy, all my will, all my genius in vain? (He had always thought himself a genius.) He remembered that recently, while on his way to Siberia, he had received a letter from Svetlogub's mother, who had reproached him very foolishly, he thought, just like a woman, for having brought her son to his death by enrolling him in the terrorist organization. When he'd received her letter, he had smiled contemptuously. What could this stupid woman understand about the goals he and Svetlogub had set before themselves? But now, remembering the letter and Svetlogub's tender, trusting, passionate personality, he thought about Svetlogub—and about himself. Perhaps his whole life had been a mistake. He closed his eyes, wanting to fall asleep, but instead he felt the same terrible feeling he had felt in his first month at St. Peter-and-Paul's Fortress—the same pain in the back of his head, the same huge terrible faces, mouths covered with fur, terrible faces on a dark background with stars. And then smaller figures, which stood before him even though his eyes were open. Now there was something new, as well—a convict in dark pants with a shaved head was flying above him. And Mezhenetsky found himself once again looking for a ventilation grate where he could fasten the rope.

Unbearable anger and hatred burned in his heart, and that hatred had to manifest itself somehow. He could not sit in one place; he could not calm down or distract his thoughts.

"How?" he asked himself. "What should I do? Cut my artery? No, I can't do it. Could I hang myself? Yes, that would be the simplest thing."

He remembered that there was a rope tying up a bunch of firewood, lying in the corridor.

"I could step up on the firewood or on the stool. There is a guard in the corridor. But he will either fall asleep or go out for a break. I will wait until he goes, and then bring the rope into my cell and tie it to the ventilation grate."

Standing by his door, Mezhenetsky listened to the steps of the prison guard in the corridor. Sometimes when the guard went to the furthest end of the corridor, Mezhenetsky looked out the door. The prison guard neither went away nor fell asleep. Mezhenetsky listened eagerly to the noise made by the guard's steps and waited.

At that moment, in another prison cell, there was a sick old man, lying in darkness cut only by a small, smoky lamp. Surrounded by the noises of sleeping people, their snoring and moaning and coughing, one of the greatest things in the world was taking place. The Old Believer was dying, and the eyes of his spirit could see everything he had sought during all of his life. In the midst of a great blinding light, he saw a lamb in the form of a transfigured young man, and a great multitude of people from all nations stood before the young man in white robes. Everyone rejoiced, and there was no longer any evil on earth. The old man knew that all this took place both in his soul and in all the world, and he felt great joy and peace.

The people who shared the old man's cell saw a very different picture. They saw the old man moaning in the agony of death. His neighbor awoke first, and he woke the others. Then the moaning stopped, and the old man became quiet and cold. And when it was over, his cell mates began to knock at the cell door.

The prison guard opened the door and went in. Ten minutes later, two prisoners carried out the dead body and took it down to the morgue. The prison guard went out with them, closing the door behind him. The corridor was empty.

Yes, yes, lock the door, lock the door, thought Mezhenetsky, watching everything that was going on from behind the door of his cell. *But you will not stop me from escaping all this absurd horror.*

Mezhenetsky no longer felt that inner horror which had tormented him until now. He was entirely obsessed with one thought, and nothing could deter him from carrying out his intention.

With his heart pounding, he went to the bunch of tied wood, untied the rope, and pulled it out from the wood. Watching the door at the end of the corridor, he brought the rope back to his cell. There he climbed on his stool and tied the middle of the rope around the ventilation grate. When he brought the two ends of the rope together, he tested the knot, then made a noose from the doubled rope. The loop was too low. He tied the rope higher, made the noose again, and then tried it on his neck. Nervously listening and glancing at the door the entire time, he climbed the stool, stuck his head into the noose, tightened it, and then pushed away the stool.

The prison guard found Mezhenetsky during his morning rounds. The guard saw that Mezhenetsky was standing almost on his feet, with his knees bent, next to the overturned stool. They pulled him out of the noose. The chief officer came. When he found out that Roman was a doctor, they sent for him, so that he could render some medical assistance to this man who had committed suicide.

They tried all the usual ways to revive him, but Mezhenetsky did not respond.

His body was carried down to the morgue, and they laid it on the tiles next to the body of the Old Believer.

THE REQUIREMENTS OF LOVE

THE REQUIREMENTS OF LOVE

Let us imagine a couple, a man and a woman—either a husband and wife, or a brother and sister, or a father and daughter, or a mother and son—who belong to the upper class and who understand the sins of their idle and luxurious life. Imagine that, after living in the midst of the poverty of the oppressed, they left the city, somehow got rid of their excessive property, and kept only a moderate income for themselves in the bank—say 150 rubles a year for two people—or maybe even left nothing for themselves, and earn their living by means of some craft, such as painting porcelain or translating good writers. They live in a Russian village in the countryside, in a log cabin they have rented or purchased, and they work with their own hands in the garden and the orchard and take care of bees, and they provide the local villagers with medical assistance, teach their children, and write personal and official letters for them.

What could be better?

But this kind of life would quickly cease being happy unless these people could refrain from lying and hypocrisy and try to be completely sincere. After all, this couple gave up all the advantages, pleasures, and adornments of the life they had enjoyed in the city, when they had money, because they realized that all people are their brothers, equal before their heavenly Father—unequal in abilities and qualities, perhaps, but equal in their right to life and to anything they might achieve in life.

Although one might hesitate regarding the equality of one adult in comparison to another, we can clearly see the equality of all humanity when we observe children. Why is it that one child may have all the care and help he needs for his mental and physical development, but another child with the same or even better potential may get rickets, or maggots, or develop some other disability because of a lack of mother's milk or of other nourishment, so that he matures without proper education and ends up an uncultivated adult filled with prejudices, useful only for rude physical labor? Why does this happen?

The reason this couple left the city and went to live in the village as they did was because they believed—not in word only, but in deed as well—in the brotherhood of humanity, and they wanted to live out this ideal not in general, theoretical terms, but in their own real, particular lives. And their attempt to accomplish this—if they are completely sincere—must inescapably bring them into a terrible situation.

With the habits acquired in their childhood—habits of order, comfort, and most importantly, cleanliness—they came to the village and rented or acquired a log cabin, exterminated the insects, perhaps painted it or covered the walls with new wallpaper, and added a few simple and necessary pieces of furniture: an iron bed, a wardrobe, a writing table. And so they live. At first, the locals seem wild and keep them at a distance. Feeling suspicious of the newcomers, as they do of all wealthy people, they try to guard themselves from the couple's advances. Eventually, a feeling of understanding begins to develop, and the position of the visitors improves. They are always ready to serve their neighbors without payment, and the most courageous and perspicacious of the villagers learn that these newcomers never refuse, so the villagers should profit as much as possible from their presence.

Their neighbors begin asking them for assistance. With time, they become more demanding in their requests.

Some do not simply ask or beg for favors, but demand a share of their surplus of material possessions. These two people who chose to live in the village among the simple people feel an obligation to share their abundance with those who live in extreme need. Eventually, if they continually give and give to the others, they will have the same amount the others have—that is, the same amount an average person has. (But who is this average person? We have no clear definition.) The newcomers cannot stop giving, because the two of them have more than the other people who live around them in glaring need. It seems to them that they should keep a glass of milk for themselves—but Matryona, their neighbor, has two children; one is a nursing infant who cannot get enough milk from her mother's breast, and the other is a two-year-old who is on the brink of starvation. It seems to them that they should keep a pillow and a blanket in order to sleep normally after the working day—but here is a sick villager who sleeps on a very old caftan instead of a mattress, who shivers from cold at night, covering himself with a shabby, moth-eaten blanket. It seems to them that they need some tea or some food—but they have to give it to the pilgrims, weak and old, who come to their door. It seems that they should at least preserve the cleanliness of their house, but the poor children come and stay overnight, and they bring lice and insects with them.

The couple cannot stop. At what point could they stop?

Only those who do not understand the feeling of universal brotherhood that caused these two people to move to the village, and also those who habitually lie, would be unable to perceive the difference between the truth and the lie and would say that a point exists at which these two could stop. The truth is that there is no such limit, that the feeling for the sake of which they are doing all this has no limits. If it has a limit, then this means that they never possessed this feeling, and acted in hypocrisy.

Continuing my description: These two people work all day, and afterwards come home, but they have neither bed nor pillow. They have to sleep on raw straw which they got somewhere, and after eating some bread they go to sleep. It is autumn, and an icy rain is falling outside. Someone knocks at the door. Can they refuse to open it? A man enters; he is soaked to the skin and feverish. What should they do? Should they let him enter and allow him to lie down on their dry straw? But there is no dry straw to spare. They must either turn the sick man away, or bring him in and let him sleep wet on the bare floor—or give him their own straw, and then lie down somewhere else themselves, perhaps even beside him, because you have to sleep somewhere. But this is not all: another man comes whom you know to be a dissipated drunkard because he has borrowed money from you on several previous occasions, and spent it all on drink each time. With quivering lips he asks for three more rubles—the amount he has stolen from his friends and spent on drink, and for which he will be sent to prison if he does not repay them.

You tell him that you have only four rubles and that you need to pay your bills tomorrow, but the man who came to you says, "All that you say is just words, and when it comes to deeds you are just like everyone else—let another person die, even though we call him 'a brother,' just so long as we take care of ourselves?"

What shall you do? How shall you behave? Should you put this feverish man on the damp floor, and keep the dry straw for yourself? This is no good—you will be unable to fall asleep. But if you take him into your bed and lie down next to him, you will get lice and maybe even typhoid. If you give this man who asks you for money these last three rubles, you will be without bread tomorrow. But to deny him means that what he says is true: you reject everything you have claimed to live for. If you can stop at this point, then why didn't you stop before? Why did you relinquish your property and leave the city? Why did you give all your possessions away to these people? Why did you help them before? Where is the limit? And if there is a limit to the things you were doing, then the whole thing is meaningless—or has only one terrible meaning: hypocrisy.

How should we behave? What should we do? Not to stop means to destroy your life, to rot, to wither away, to die, and this seems a senseless, useless death. To stop halfway means to admit you were wrong, to renounce your beliefs, for the sake of which you did everything you have done, for which you tried to do something good. But you can't renounce these beliefs because it is the truth that we are brothers and that we should serve each other. It was not invented by me, nor even by Christ. It is simply true, and once this idea is inside of someone, you cannot remove the consciousness of it from his heart.

What then should we do? Is there any way out?

Let us imagine that these two people, rather than being frightened away by the situation that their sacrifice has placed them in, decide that this hardship came about because the means with which they came to help people were too small, and that it wouldn't be this way and they could be of more use if they had more money. Imagine that they find another source of assistance that enables them to collect large, or even huge, sums of money in order to help people. Even so, in less than a week, the same situation would repeat itself. Very soon, all the resources, no matter how great, would be poured into the myriad of tiny holes created by poverty, and things would remain the same.

But perhaps there is a third way out. There are people who say that the answer is to promote universal education, and inequality will disappear.

But this solution is hypocritical. You cannot educate a population that perpetually lives on the brink of starvation. And, more importantly, the insincerity of the people who promote this idea is seen in this: Those who propose to establish equality through education and science still support the existing inequality in their own comfortable lives.

But there is still a fourth solution: to destroy the causes of this inequality, destroy the violence that created it.

This solution can't help but enter the minds of those sincere people who want to fulfill in their lives the principle of universal brotherhood.

"If we cannot live here among the people in this village," this couple whom I earlier imagined might say, "and if we have been placed in such a terrible situation that we are bound to rot, wither away, and die, or else renounce the only moral basis of our lives, then this is the cause of our dilemma: some people are rich and others are poor. And this inequality is the result of violence, and therefore we must resist violence." Only by bringing an end to this violence and the slavery that results from it can we make it possible to serve people without having to sacrifice our lives.

But how can you destroy this violence? Where is it? It is in a soldier, in a policeman, in a village counselor, in the lock that seals my door. How can I fight this violence? By what means? Should we fight like those who live by violence and who use violence against violence?

No. For a sincere and honest person, that is impossible. To fight violence with violence means merely to replace the old violence with new violence. To collect money obtained by violence and then give it to people who were robbed by means of violence means, again, to cure the wounds created by violence by means of yet more violence.

Therefore you must fight not with more violence, but rather by means of preaching nonviolence and love—and, most importantly, by being a living example of nonviolence and sacrifice, because for a Christian in this world who wants to fight violence, there is no more effective way than by sacrifice, and sacrifice right to the end.

A person may not find in himself the strength and determination to jump into this abyss, but those who are sincere and want to obey the law of God that they understand in their conscience, cannot avoid fulfilling this duty. You can decide not to make this sacrifice, but if you want to fulfill the requirements of love, you must give your whole life, and not deceive yourself.

But this sacrifice is not as awful as it seems, because the bottom of humanity's need is not as deep as it seems. Perhaps we respond to its call like the young boy who hung all night from the edge of the well, clinging only with his hands. When at last he fell, terrified of the deep water he imagined in the well, the boy discovered that, only two feet below him, the bottom of the well was dry.

SISTERS

SISTERS

I

On the third of May, 1882, a three-masted sailing ship, "Our Lady of Winds," sailed from Havre to the Chinese Sea. It unloaded its cargo in China, took on a new cargo which it brought to Buenos Aires, and from there carried another cargo to Brazil.

All of these journeys, along with damages, repairs, months of dead calm, winds that pushed the ship off course, and other delays and misfortunes slowed the ship so much and so often that it was not until May 8, 1886, that she arrived in Marseilles with a cargo of boxes of American canned goods.

When the ship left Havre, it had a captain, a first mate, and fourteen sailors. During the voyage one sailor died, four disappeared in various adventures, and only nine of the original sailors returned to France. To replace the lost sailors, the captain had hired some additional crew: two Americans, a Negro, and a Swede they had found in a small restaurant in a port in Singapore.

The sails were furled and the rigging and tackle were tied to the masts. A tugboat came and, with engines straining noisily, pulled the ship into the harbor in line with the other ships. The sea was calm; only near the shore were there slight ripples splashing. Many other sailing ships from every country in the world were anchored in the port. They were big and small, of all shapes and sizes and with various types of rigging. "Our Lady of Winds" stood between an Italian brig and a British merchant ship, each of which moved slightly aside to make room for their new companion.

As soon as the captain had finished with the customs and port officials, he allowed half of the crew to go ashore overnight.

It was a warm summer night. The streets of Marseilles were all lit up. The smell of food wafted from the kitchens, and the sounds of conversations, noisy carriage wheels, and happy shouts came from all directions.

The crew of "Our Lady of Winds" had not stood on solid ground for four months, and after they went ashore they walked along the city streets humbly, as foreigners, as people who were unaccustomed to city life. They looked around them and smelled the city night as if they were searching for something. They had not seen a woman for four months and they were tortured by lust.

A tall, intelligent, muscular fellow named Celestine Duclos took the lead, as he always did when they went ashore. He could always find good places to visit, and he did not start fistfights, as often happens to sailors when they go ashore; but even if such a fight started, he could stand up for himself and would never hide behind his friends.

The sailors pushed through the dark streets that all led down to the sea and carried the rotten smells of old basements and pantries. Finally, Celestine chose a small, narrow alley lit by large lanterns above the doors, and followed it. The sailors followed him, singing and joking. Huge street numbers were painted on the translucent glass of the lanterns. Women in aprons sat on straw chairs along the street in front of narrow doors. When they saw the sailors, they jumped up, ran into the middle of the street, and lured them into their dens.

From time to time, in the depth of some corridor, a door flung open and a half-dressed woman appeared, wearing tight cotton pants, a short skirt, and a dark velvet top cut low to show the golden lace underneath. "Hey, handsome boys, come on in!"

Sometimes such a woman would run out into the street and glue herself to a sailor, like a spider capturing a fly stronger than herself, as she tried to pull him through her door. The lustful sailor would offer some weak resistance, and the others would stand by to see what would happen. But Celestine Duclos would cry, "No, not here, don't go in. We're going further." And the boy would listen and drag himself out of the woman's embraces.

The sailors went further and further, followed by the scolding of the disappointed women. When the other women further along the street heard the noise that followed the men, they leapt from their doorways and they, too, glued themselves to the sailors and praised their merchandise in husky voices. Thus they went further. Sometimes they ran into a group of soldiers, or maybe a middle-class citizen or a shop assistant, sneaking away to their usual spots. The same kind of lanterns were burning on other streets, but the sailors walked further and further, stepping through the wastewater that flowed from beneath these houses filled with female bodies. Then Celestine Duclos stopped in front of one of the houses that looked a little better than others and led his group inside.

II

The sailors sat down in a huge hall of the pub. Each man picked a girl for himself and did not part with her until the end of the evening; this was the rule of the house. Three tables were moved together. First the sailors drank wine with the women, and then they went upstairs. The large, heavy shoes of twenty feet pounded up the wooden steps, then pushed through the narrow doors and dispersed among the bedrooms. From the bedrooms they went downstairs again for a drink, and then back upstairs, and so on, repeating the cycle several times.

Their revelry reached amazing heights. The sailors spent six months of salary in four hours of debauchery. By eleven o'clock in the evening, they were all drunk, and with bloodshot eyes, they shouted incoherently, not knowing what they were saying. Each of them had a woman on his lap. Someone was singing, someone shouting; someone was smashing his fist on the table, someone pouring wine down his throat.

Celestine Duclos was sitting among his friends. He, too, had a woman on his knees, a rather plump girl with pink cheeks. He had drunk no less than the others, but he was not completely drunk; he still had some thoughts moving through his head. He was indulging himself and trying to sustain a conversation with his girlfriend. But his thoughts came and went, and he could not seem to catch and gather them long enough to express himself.

Laughing, he said, "Well, well—how long have you been here?"

"Six months," the girl answered.

He nodded, as if he approved. "And tell me now, do you like it?"

She thought for a while, then said, "I've got used to it. You have to make a living somehow. This is better than working as a servant or at the laundry."

He nodded again, as if approving. "And you aren't from around here, are you?"

She shook her head.

"Are you from far away?"

She nodded.

"From where?"

She thought for a second, as if trying to remember. "From Perpignan," she said.

"Well, well," he said, and then he remained silent for a while.

"And who are you, are you a sailor?" she asked.

"Yes, we are sailors," he answered.

"Have you been far away?"

"Yes, very far. We saw all kinds of things."

"Did you go around the world?"

"Not just once, but twice."

She stopped, as if she were trying to remember something.

"And probably you've met many other ships, haven't you?" she asked.

"What do you think?"

"Have you, by any chance, met 'Our Lady of Winds'? Is there such a ship?"

He was surprised that she had named his ship, but he decided to joke with her. "Sure. We met that ship last week."

"Is that true?" she asked, becoming pale.

"Yes, it's true."

"You're not lying to me, are you?"

"I swear to God," he said.

"And did you meet a man named Celestine Duclos?"

"Celestine Duclos?" He repeated, startled and even a bit frightened. *How could she know my name?* he wondered. And she seemed to be afraid of something. "How do you know him?"

"No, it's not me, but there is a woman here who knows him."

"Which woman? From this house?"

"No. From around here."

"Where exactly is 'from around here'?"

"Not far."

"And who is this woman?"

"Just a woman. Like me."

"And what does she want with him?"

"How should I know? Maybe they both came from the same city."

They looked straight into each other's eyes.

"I would like to see this woman," he said.

"Why? Do you want to tell her something?"

"I want to tell her that I saw Celestine Duclos."

"You met him? Is he alive? Is he healthy?"

"Yes, he's in good health. Why?"

She was silent for a while as if collecting her thoughts, and then she said quietly, "And where is 'Our Lady of Winds' going now?"

"Where? To Marseilles."

"Is that true?" she cried.

"Yes, it's true."

"And you know Duclos?"

"I told you, I know him."

She thought for a while. "Yes, yes, this is good," she said quietly. "Why do you want him?"

"If you see him, please tell him . . . no, you'd better not."

"What?"

"Nothing, just nothing."

He looked at her, becoming increasingly worried.

"I think that you must know him. Do you know him?"

"No, I don't."

"Then why are you asking about this fellow?"

Without answering, she suddenly jumped off his knee, went to the small bar where the madam sat, took a lemon, cut it in two pieces, squeezed some juice into a glass, added some water, and gave it to Celestine.

"Here, drink this," she said, and returned to his lap.

"Why should I?" he asked, taking the glass from her.

"It'll cut the alcohol. You have to be less drunk. I'll tell you in a few minutes. Drink."

He drank the glass and wiped his lips with the sleeve of his shirt. "Now tell me your story. I'm listening."

"And you will not tell him that you saw me here? Or that you heard it from me?"

"All right. I won't tell him."

"Swear to God!"

He swore.

"Did you swear to God?"

"Yes, I swore to God."

"Then tell him that his father and his mother and his brother have all died. They had a fever, and in one month all three of them died."

Duclos felt that suddenly all his blood pushed into his heart. For several minutes he sat without saying anything—he did not know what to say—and then he spoke: "And you know this for sure?"

"For sure."

"Who told you this?"

She put her arms around his shoulders and looked directly into his eyes.

"Swear to God that you won't tell this secret to anyone."

"I swear to God."

"I am his sister."

"Françoise?" he cried.

She looked at him carefully, with her full attention, and then her lips moved quietly, barely getting the words out. "So it's you, Celestine."

They did not move, but sat frozen, looking into each other's eyes.

Around them the others were shouting in drunken voices. They heard the sounds of glasses shattering, palms slapping, heavy shoes stomping, and the piercing shrieks of women, all mixed together.

"How can this be?" he said very quietly, so softly that he could hardly hear his own words.

Her eyes were suddenly filled with tears. "Yes, they all died, all three of them in one month. And what could I do? I was left alone. To pay the money we owed to the pharmacist and to the doctor, and to pay for the funeral for three of them, I sold everything we had, and I had to carry on without anything, not a single cent. So I went to work as a servant to the landlord Cashen— you remember, he was a lame man. I was only fifteen years old. When you left, I wasn't even fourteen. I fell into sin with him— we women are foolish. Then I went to work as a nurse in the home of a notary. He did the same thing to me. For a while I lived as his mistress in a small rented apartment. Then he abandoned me, and for three days I had nothing to eat. Nobody would take me in. So I came here, as others have."

As she talked, tears flowed steadily from her eyes and nose, down her cheeks and into her mouth.

"What have we done? What a terrible thing we have done!" he said.

"I thought that you had already died too," she whispered through her tears. "Do you think that I wanted this?"

"But why didn't you recognize me?" he asked, also in a whisper.

"I don't know! It's not my fault!" she insisted, and cried even harder.

"Do you think I could have recognized you? You were not like this when I left. But how could you not recognize me?" he said.

She shook in her head in despair. "Well, I see so many men here that they all look the same to me."

His heart was wrung so painfully that he wanted to shout, or to bellow like a small boy who has been beaten. He stood, lifted her from his lap, and then caught her head in his huge sailor's paws and looked very carefully at her face.

Slowly, he recognized in this face the face of the happy, skinny little girl he had left at home with those whose eyes she had closed for the last time. "Yes, yes, you are Françoise. You are my sister!" he murmured.

And suddenly the sobs, the deep sobs of a man which are like the hiccups of a drunkard, rose in his throat. He let her head go, and then he hit the table with his fist so hard that the glasses jumped and fell over, and he shouted in a loud, wild voice.

His friends stared at him.

"Look at him, he's drunk," said one of them.

"Stop shouting! Hey!" another said.

"Hey, Duclos, why are you making all this noise? Let's go upstairs again," the third man said, pulling Celestine's sleeve with one hand and with the other embracing the laughing woman who sat on his knees. She had very rosy cheeks and shining eyes, and she was dressed in very low-cut pink silk lingerie.

Celestine Duclos became suddenly quiet. He held his breath and stared at his friends. Then, with the strange and resolute expression he used when in a fistfight, he, weaving from side to side, turned toward the sailor who was embracing the girl and thrust his hands between them, separating them. "Get away from her! Can't you see that she's your sister? They're all somebody's sisters! And here is Françoise—she too is a sister! Ha-ha-ha!"

He began weeping, but it looked like laughter. His body was listing from side to side, and suddenly, with a crash, he fell face down on the floor. He rolled around, beating the floor with his hands and legs, shouting hoarsely and wheezing like a dying man.

"We should put him to bed," one of his friends said. "Otherwise, if he goes outside, the police might take him in."

So they took Celestine upstairs to Françoise's bedroom and put him in her bed.

A NOTE ON THE TYPE

This book was set in Adobe Caslon, a revival of the original typeface cut and designed by William Caslon in the 1720s and 1730s. The typeface had both immediate and long-term success due to its exceptional readability and friendly charm. Caslon began his career as an engraver of pistols and musket locks. His skill of precision in intricate engravings led him to the art of letter-founding. His improvement to the quality of type has led some to say that he changed the course of printing history. The ornaments in this book are also modeled after original designs by William Caslon.

Book design and composition by
Laura Klynstra Blost

Printed and bound by
R. R. Donnelley & Sons,
Crawfordsville, Indiana

We want to hear from you. Please send your comments about this
book to us in care of the address below. Thank you.

ZondervanPublishingHouse
Grand Rapids, Michigan 49530
http://www.zondervan.com